# Cherry Hill Love Affair

## Ryan Hodge

SMP
PUBLISHING

SMP Publishing Edition

Printed in the United States of America

10 9 8 7 6 5 4 3 2 1

ISBN: 978-0-9977990-7-1 (PBK)

# DEDICATION

To my mother who I miss so much, I remember walking down the street, your hand I would touch.

Years have passed since you've been physically with us, would give a fortune to hear your voice, even if it was a fuss.

Our times I will forever hold dear in my heart, I could list them forever in a never-ending chart.

I still live life lessons that you taught me, they made life easier and glee they brought me.

I thank you for all the love, and I still feel it from the heavens above.

I love you forever Ma.

# CHAPTER 1

"Niggas, it's money out here tonight! Fucking fiends all over. I already G'd off tonight and I just got on da block like two hours ago. Them muhfuckers know my shit is bonkers," I say.

"Hell yeah, nigga. They been up and down Lincoln Street all fucking night. I ran outta shit before you got out here. Shit been selling nonstop all night. I started to leave the block since I ran outta shit, but then you pulled up," AK mentions.

"Word. Son, I got plenty of shit, so it look like I'm gonna be out here all night. You might as well help me pump this shit. We fuck around and get rid of all of it," I respond.

"That's what it is. Yo, you know I'm down. It's money out here and I'm damn sure trying to get it. We fuck around and break day getting this paper," AK voices.

I speak, "For sure. I was gonna take ole girl to the motel and get a short stay, but that shit is over nigga. We definitely getting this money."

"I hope the fuckin pigs don't run up on the block fucking with us. We just trying to get ours. Them bastards just mad that we getting more money than them. Hate the fucking pigs. I probably made them niggas' monthly salary since I been on the block today," AK utters.

"Yo son, you know they stay running down and don't be finding shit. They only making like thirty grand a year. We definitely made their weekly salary already. Them niggas dumb as hell," I word.

"Why you say they dumb as hell?" asks Big D.

I answer, "I say anybody who works is dumb. Son, check this out. All these mother fuckers go to work for forty or fifty hours a week and be broke as hell. They get a check and pay everybody else and then barely have enough dough left over to enjoy."

AK chimes in, "Hell yeah. And they slaves to the clock. Gotta wake up early as hell and go run to a job and do what the white man tells them to do. Sitting in corny ass meetings around people they don't even like. Fuck dat! I ain't no nine to five nigga. I'm gonna hug da block like I hug my mom dukes on Mother's Day."

"True, I feel where you coming from, but Rah, you work at a job though," Big D says.

"Yeah man I do, but that's just a front. I just use it for tax purposes. That being broke shit is for the birds. We on da block moving how we wanna move. Besides, I work like three, four hours a day. It's all part of a bigger purpose," I orate.

Big D responds, "No doubt. I see you're on ya shit!"

I shoot back, "Hell yeah! I'm always on point. I'm like a sniper with this getting money shit."

AK orders, "Well, get on point and roll the fucking dice nigga or give them shits up or something. Damn, you holding them shits like a mom holding a newborn."

AK has already lost six hundred dollars to me and Big D is down about the same amount. I'm killing these niggas tonight. When you're hot, you're hot and I'm molten lava tonight. I've had the bank since I got to the block and they can't win it back. It's only three hundred in the bank now because I keep rolling "Cee-lo" and emptying that shit out. I'd be up more paper if the fiends didn't keep interrupting our game.

I love rolling Cee-lo. Every night we're on the block we play this shit. I love gambling just as much as I love hustling. I think it's the rush I get from it. Most stuff in life is so predictable and fake, but not this. You never know what's going to happen out here on Lincoln Street. It seems like there is never a dull moment on the block. Regular life isn't for me. It's too much like somebody wrote a script and people just follow it. I love the action of the nightlife of a nigga getting money.

We're out here getting mad paper, fucking bitches, and getting high. Well, I don't smoke, but my boys do. I'm only 19 years old and have about ninety-grand buried in St. Marks Park. That's not all of my dough because I even have money at my crib and a nice stash in a safety deposit box down south. I'm young, black, and I'm getting it.

"Fuck you AK. I'm gonna roll this dice again and take more of y'all niggas' money. I'm surprised y'all ain't quit yet," I state.

I roll the dice and roll trips. I'm on fire for real. We are paying double for trips, so they have to pay me. Big D pays me and calls it a night. He's tired of losing his money and it's late, so he dips off. It's just me and AK now going head-to-head. I know as long as he has money he'll keep playing. AK hates losing just as much as I do and will not quit as long as he's breathing. While we're rolling dice, fiends keep coming to the block to get served and we keep serving them.

A few hours later, I'm down to my last clip. AK is done playing dice, so we just post up on the block to see if I can get this last clip off. It's taking a little longer than I want to wait for a fiend to come through, so we decide to bounce. Besides, it's already five thirty in the morning and

I'm tired as hell. Just as we're going to leave another fiend comes up.

"You straight?" she asks.

"Yeah, what you want?" I inquire.

"Let me get two clips," she answers as she rubs her neck.

That's good shit! I can finish this shit with this one last sale. I love nights like tonight. The money has been flowing incessantly. I made so much tonight that I might disappear from the block for a few days. I might run back down south or something.

"I only have one clip left and I ain't taking no shorts. I'm letting you know what it is. If you want it, I'll be right back," I answer.

The fiend lets me know she'll take the one clip and I step off to go get it. I grab the last clip out of my stash on the tracks and start making my way back to Lincoln Street. I'm getting closer to Lincoln Street when I see somebody move inside a car that's parked on the block. Why the hell is a couple of white men sitting in the car at five something in the morning over here? It also ain't sittin well with me that the fiend asked for two clips. She never has asked for that much before and I've been serving her for about a year now. Not to mention, she always asks for shorts when she cops from me.

You know what? That rat ass fiend is trying to set me up! That's the police sitting in that fucking car! They were either going to do a buy and bust or get her to cop from me to indict me later. I do the call that me and my boys have to alert them that there is police presence. When I do the call, AK picks his head up and goes to jump in his car. I turn around and go the opposite direction back towards the tracks. Two seconds later the car that was parked speeds out of the parking space and heads in my direction doing what seems like a hundred miles per hour. Another patrol car comes from the direction of the tracks.

Shit! I can't drop this clip right here because they'll see me for sure. I decide to keep the clip and outrun the cops. They're all fat doughnut eaters and I'm in the best shape of my life. They'll never be able to catch me. I run across the street and jump the fence into Lincoln Street Park. The foot race is on. Who will win me or them? As I'm running, I look back and see two patrol cars have cornered AK's car and have him blocked in. They have guns drawn on him and he couldn't get out of dodge if he wanted to.

I make it through the park and cross Curtis Street in less time than it takes to blink. One officer has jumped out of his patrol car and is on foot chasing me, but I have a great lead on him. The other cop stays in his car and is driving around the block to possibly cut me off on Middlesex Street. I'm sure he expects to catch me crossing Middlesex Street. I don't care if they catch me at some point as long as I get this clip off me.

I get into the backyards of the houses bordering Curtis and Middlesex Street. I know these backyards like I know my own bedroom. I know the cops can't see me in the darkness of the backyards and decide to throw the clip as far away from me as possible, but the cop who is chasing me on foot is closer than I thought. If he sees me throw the drugs, he'll easily know where to find them if they catch me. Damn, I have to keep running with the shit on me.

I cut through the backyards of the houses between Curtis Street and Middlesex Street. I hope the cop in the patrol car hasn't made it on to Middlesex Street yet because he'll see me crossing the street, but I can't stop running now because I still have the cop on foot chasing me and the clip is still in my pocket. I run across Middlesex Street in a quick flash as if I'm a deer running from a lion on a prairie. My luck is not as good as it was when I was playing dice because the cop in the patrol car has made it to the exact spot where I'm crossing Middlesex Street. Unfortunately, I don't have the luxury of stopping, so I do the only thing I can do. I summon all the strength I have in my body and jump onto the hood of the cop car.

I don't slow down one bit and actually keep right in stride as I disappear into the backyards of the houses on the other side of Middlesex Street. The cop car being in the street helps me out a great deal because it slows down the cop behind me enough to give me a little more breathing room. He's not as athletically inclined as I am. He runs around the front of the patrol unit and continues his pursuit. I still don't have enough clearance to drop or throw the clip without being detected, so I come up with another plan to get rid of the shit.

I take the rubber band off the clip as I continue to run through the backyards. I figure it'll be impossible to find each individual bottle in the darkness of the night, so I toss the bottles as I'm running. I don't make it obvious that I'm tossing the bottles while I'm running. It looks as if I'm just pumping my arms running as a track runner does in the straight away. I arrive in the backyards of the houses bordering Henry Street on the next block, but I don't run to the street. Instead, I run through more backyards in an effort to discard a couple more bottles. Through my efforts, I've gotten rid of four of the vials. I decide to cross Henry Street and see the worst sight of my life. The police have the street blocked off and I don't see how I can get away. I don't see the cop who was on my heels anymore, so I dip down behind a car in the driveway of a house on Henry Street.

While I'm ducked down behind the car, I plan my next move. I get overtaken by a great idea. I take off running again into the middle of the street. Of course, the police chase after me like I'm Harrison Ford in the "Fugitive". Unfortunately, there are too many of them for me to elude and I'm tired as hell from all of the running and fence jumping. I do make it to the backyard of a house on Passaic Ave. which is one more block over.

Three cops are squatting in the backyard of a house and one tackles me as soon as I enter the yard. The cop tackles me like he's an NFL linebacker. He knocks me off of my feet and about five feet into the air. I was already out of breath from all the police evading, but the officer manages to knock more breath out of me from his heroic tackle. A second after getting tackled, I have a knee on my neck from one cop, another cop yanking my arms, and the third cop has his gun pointing at me.

"Give me your hands, asshole," one officer orders.

I comply with his order because I don't want to get any unnecessary charges. Additionally, I don't want to get beat down or maybe even shot from resisting arrest. Let's face it, there are three cops and just me in this backyard. I know they can do whatever they want to me in this instance and nothing will happen to them. They're already mad that I made them run after me. Being equipped with this information makes me relax and comply. The cops rough me up a little bit, cuff my hands, and tie my feet with plastic zip ties. I guess they don't want me to run again.

They drag me out of the backyard to the street where many other officers are. It's a summer night and I have on shorts, so my legs are getting scraped up from them being dragged on the ground. I definitely want to steal off on a couple of these pigs, but I can't. The police officers dragging me finally get me to a patrol car and slam me forcefully on the hood of the car. My face smashes against the hood of the car with so much force that the blow slightly dazes me. I know they are heated that I took them on a chase around the neighborhood. The way I see it is that they chose to come after me. I didn't ask for it, so they shouldn't be mad at me. In all reality they should be mad at themselves.

As I'm slightly dazed, I feel the cops tugging at my pockets. They flip my pockets inside out to the point that they look like rabbit ears. They place all the contents of my pockets on the top of the car. My money, keys, chapstick, and rubbers are all on the roof of the car. Next, one of the cops starts to pat me down. I'm upset because I can barely breathe from all of the pressure they're putting on my neck as they hold me down, so I start squirming. The cop assumes I'm squirming because he's getting close to the drugs that he thinks I have on me.

As they continue patting me down, they realize that I don't have anything on me and become upset. One cop applies more pressure to my neck to be spiteful. They know they can stop restraining me because I'm tied up on my legs and arms. I'm still shaking off the impact of my head being rammed against the car when they start questioning me.

"Where you put the drugs at Ray?" one officer asks.

I don't respond because I'm still groggy from the blow to the head and I'm winded from all the running and fence jumping. The police officer asks me the same question again except this time he asks more angrily and aggressively. The pigs even fondle my dick and check my ass crack to see if I'm hiding the drugs there. Finally, I'm clear headed and begin to catch my breath.

I answer, "I ain't got no fucking drugs."

"Bullshit! You went to the tracks to get something to give to that lady. Make this easy for us and we'll let you go. You won't have to be delayed much longer," a cop says to coerce me to rat myself out.

These cops kill me. They must think I'm dumb as hell. There's no way in hell that if I tell on myself, they will let me go. I'm just going to keep my mouth shut and let them prove what they think they know. One cop grabs me by my throat forcefully and berates me as if I'm a child. Several of the officers walk away from me and begin searching for the drugs that I dumped. They'll be searching for hours and will be lucky to find even one of the vials of crack I dropped. I just hope they cut me loose sometime this year.

The scene on Henry Street is like something out of a movie. The police lights are speckling the darkness of the night. My ribs are starting to ache from the pummeling I received in the backyard of that house. I begin growing impatient because they've had me delayed for at least an hour now.

"Yo, y'all letting me go? You thought I was playing dumb about not having any drugs," I ask.

"Shut the hell up! We'll let you go free if and when we feel like it. Until then, just shut your ass up! We know you had drugs on you," the officer answers.

"This is some bullshit! I'm trying to tell you that I don't know what you talking about. The other cops been looking for an hour and haven't found anything. Ain't shit to find," I verbalize.

"Ray, you're nineteen years old and have three thousand dollars on you. Come on man, we're not assholes. That money you have on you is drug money. Just come clean and stop wasting everybody's time," the officer states.

I respond adamantly, "I don't sell drugs. I got that money from work. I don't go to work five days a week to sell drugs. If I could get three thousand dollars from selling drugs, I'd just do that and say fuck work."

The cop starts laughing and even summons another officer over to me, so I can repeat what I just told him. I do as he asks and I tell the next officer that I got three thousand dollars from working. Unfortunately, he doesn't believe me either and they both laugh at me.

"I don't even make three grand a month and I'm thirty-nine years old. There's no way in hell that I'm going to believe that you're nineteen and you make three thousand dollars at one time," one cop says.

The other cop asks in a patronizing fashion, "Where do you work that pays so much? Let me guess, you work for your uncle who pays you under the table?"

I respond, "No, I work in the airport and I only make a couple hundred dollars a week because I'm in school, so I don't work that many hours."

The cop cuts me off from finishing my explanation. They both give each other a look as if I'm telling on myself the more I speak. These pigs swear they're smarter than everybody. Little do they know that I'm years ahead of where their intelligence levels are. I'm telling them exactly what I want and I know what they're thinking.

"So Ray, you work in the airport for a couple hundred bucks a week, but you have a little more than three thousand dollars on you and you want us to believe that you got it from work?" one of the officers asks.

"Yes, that's what I'm saying. Finally, you two understand me," I answer.

I'm playing these officers to the max. I know they don't believe that I've saved that much money from working a part time job that only pays a couple hundred dollars a week. The fact that they don't believe me is cool with me, but I got these bastards right where I want them.

"Do you know how many months you would have had to save up a couple hundred dollars a week to get over three thousand dollars total?" the officer asks.

I say, "No, I don't know how many months it would take, but I got most of that all in one check."

"We got you right there! You just got yourself caught in your own fucking lie. You just told us that you only make a couple hundred dollars a week and now you're telling us that you made most of the three grand we found on you in a week. Stop the fucking lying buddy," one cop voices excitedly.

"Man, I'm not lying. I got most of that money from my job for tuition reimbursement. They pay my college tuition over at Montclair State as long as I pass my classes. They gave me a check for almost three thousand dollars and the rest of the money is from my paycheck. That's why I have all of that money on me," I explain.

Their mouths drop when I explain my situation to them. They really thought they caught me in a lie, but they didn't because they are dim-witted. I dangled a little bit of bait in front of them and they took it and ran with it only to hit a brick wall. I see many of the other officers walking back to our direction.

"That must be one hell of a job," the cop says.

"I love my job because they treat their employees fairly. Listen, if you don't believe me, you can check my car. It's parked on Lincoln Street. The check stub and my work badge are both in the glove box," I speak.

One of the cops asks me which car is mine and goes to check it. They still have me restrained, but I know I'll be released soon. The other cops who went searching for the drugs return empty-handed as I suspected they would. About ten minutes later, the cop who went to my car to retrieve the check stub for my tuition reimbursement returns with exactly what I told him he would find. They are all visibly pissed about having to let me go because they know I'm dirty, but they have no evidence. Their buy and bust tactics didn't work on me. They tell me that it's not a good idea to hang out late in a high drug traffic area and that I should consider hanging out in other places. Ten minutes later they give me back all of my property including my bread and cut me loose.

I walk up Lincoln Street back to my car. To my dismay, my car is flipped seemingly inside out. All of my papers are thrown everywhere; my books are snatched out of my book bag and thrown recklessly in the car, and my duffle bag that had clothes in it are scattered throughout the trunk. The pigs always have to fuck something up.

# CHAPTER 2

I wake up after sleeping until three o'clock in the afternoon. My ribs are sore as hell from last night, but I'm good though. I'm sitting in St. Marks Park on the bleachers when I see AK pull up. He gets out the car and walks over to me.

"What's good nigga? How you make out last night?" I ask. "Fuck you been?"

AK answers, "Ain't shit. I was good last night. The police ran down on me before I could move, but I ain't have shit on me, so they didn't do shit. I just made a move real quick. Feel me. Figured I'd slide through and see what's going on. I didn't want to call your phone just in case the police had that shit."

"Word. Normal shit. Just dropped my niece off. Now, I'm just trying to finish this assignment before I head to campus," I reply. "Last night got crazy as hell, but as you see I'm good. Them bastards did hold me for a long ass time, but they ain't find shit, so they let me go. They fucked me up too. My ribs sore as fuck."

"Hell yeah. I ain't surprised they fucked you up because they slammed me and I had my hands up asap. That schoolboy-college shit ain't for me nigga, but I can't knock your hustle. I ain't trying to write no boring ass papers. Fuck that.... I'd rather make this paper," AK replies as he pulls out a wad of cash and flips through the bills.

"Bra, you know I stay on my school and work shit. If not, I wouldn't have a way to justify the money I got," I voice as I pull out my wad of cash and mimic what AK just did.

"Son, that one cop was on your ass. I was saying to myself that it wasn't looking good for you," AK mentions.

"Nigga, dude was on my ass so tight that I couldn't even launch the clip while I was running. He woulda seen me throw it for sure, so I had to hold dat shit longer than I wanted. I eventually started tossing one bottle at a time, but still had a few left when they pretty much had me cornered," I orate.

AK inquires, "Damn, so what the fuck you do? You ain't eat them shits, did you?"

I reply, "Hell no! I was ducked down behind a car and I got on some Eddie Murphy shit."

"Fuck is you talking about?" AK asks.

"I was on my Eddie Murphy shit from 'Beverly Hills Cop'. Eddie Murphy put a banana in the tailpipe of the police car. While I was ducked behind the car and knew the cop that was chasing me would be on me any second, I reached down and put the other vials I had in the tailpipe of the car in the driveway and then kept running," I narrate.

"Yo, that's smart and funny as hell! The banana in the tailpipe," AK says while laughing.

We both laugh as we battle to see who has more cash. We keep flipping through the bills and it appears that we have about the same amount of money on us, so we decide to stop counting and call it a tie. We always have this battle of the pockets and never have a clear-cut winner. We always carry cash because we never know when we'll need to access cash to make a move.

I always keep a legal stream of income, so I can file taxes. Having a W-2 and being seen in a work uniform helps conceal a lot of underhanded activity. The last thing I want to do is bring suspicion to myself because I don't have a job. I'm not into flashy cars and big chains, but I am into having a lot of money. The best thing to do in my line of work is to fly under the radar.

"Word, fuck that work shit. I'm out here in these streets. Nigga, I'm in these streets like potholes in Newark," AK speaks.

I respond, "You crazy as hell! You gotta be more strategic than what you talking about. Can't be out here reckless. That's what got me cut loose last night."

"Fuck all that. You do what works for you and I'll do what works for me. You know how we do," AK conveys.

"For sure," I say.

"What's good for after class and tonight? You trying to fuck wit Velocity?" AK asks.

I answer, "Shit, after class I gotta meet old boy in sunny-side to pick up that bread. Go tuck that at the stash spot, then hit the crib to get right. I'm definitely fucking with Velocity tonight. It's Friday!"

"Son, I'll ride with you to pick the bread up and then drop it off at the spot. Then when you hit the crib, I'll go see what Drea talking bout. I can meet you at Velocity later tonight," AK speaks.

"All that sounds good except for riding with me to get the dough. You know that shit ain't gonna happen. Hell nah," I comment.

"That's that bull shit Rah! If old boy tries something shady, I won't be there to help out. You'll be assed out," AK mentions.

I reply, "Yo, we been fucking wit this dude for years. He ain't on no funny shit. The most that'll happen is he'll say he ain't got the bread, but we know he got it cause he told us to come get it. You know that. You bugging fam."

"I hear you, but I would feel a whole lot better if I rode with you," AK says.

"Son, I'll pick the bread up and then we'll

meet. Do what we do and then we go from there. No need to switch shit up now, nigga I'm good," I reply.

AK and I have this conversation every time it's time for me to link up with someone to do business. It's not surprising or aggravating that we keep having the same conversation because it's just who AK is. He's the type of person who is always hyped up and can't sit still. He's always on the move seeing what he can get into.

That's actually how he got his nickname of AK. I call him AK, which stands for Always Kinetic. He's the dude who's trying to make moves in two feet of snow because it kills him to just chill and kick back. Secondly, I call him AK because he is short tempered and is quick to pop of on anyone with no notice. When he does pop off, he's deadly like an AK-47.

I'm glad he's my homie because he always has my back and I have his. I know if it's going down that he won't hesitate to get us out of the situation. AK definitely has the big brother complex, but it works for him, so I'm cool with it.

I'm the opposite of AK when speaking of personalities. I'm more rational and calculated. I don't pop of at the drop of a dime. It takes a long time for me to lose my temper. In most cases, I don't consider stuff to be that serious to lose my cool. My squad knows that I always keep it one hundred with them. It doesn't matter if it's good or bad. That's why the team calls me Rah. It stands for Rational and Honest.

AK and I have been hustling together for a couple of years now. The money we make is great, but the friendship is even better. The memories are classic and I wouldn't trade them for the world. The last couple of years have flown by, but that's how it is when you're moving and shaking. We've been in a million sticky situations and have always come out on top because the balance we have between us. Fortunately, the number of good days and nights far surpass the bad ones.

"I'm just saying that if I meet that dude one time, I'll let the mother fucker know not to fuck us over and then I'll be done," AK utters.

"Hell nah. Look nigga... You not knowing him keeps you safe. If the white boy in Sunnyside gets knocked and the pigs put pressure on him to give up the niggas he fuck wit, they can only come get me. If you meet him and he snitches, we both will be fucked," I explain.

AK replies as he pulls out his nine and cocks it, "Son, that's what I'm saying. If I go with you, I'll let him know to keep his mouth shut if shit ever pops off. Let him know that I'm fucking serious."

"Put that shit up. It's kids out here. Son, you buggin right now. Keeping in real, if dude gets knocked, he not gonna be thinking about you or me. He's gonna do what he has to do to keep from going to jail. He'd rat on us both and then there would be nobody to bail us out," I verbalize.

"Damn, you right, but fuck all that. He should fuck with both of us. We're partners in this shit," AK words.

"Yo, you right, but it's safer for us if we keep it this way. Somebody gotta have my back if shit get ugly. You know I only trust you," I comment.

"That's what's up! That's how we ride," AK says as he daps me up.

I actually wish AK could be the one who handles the business with the drugs, but that's not possible. I'd rather my name only be associated with work and school, but I can't have everything my way.

The white boy lives in the Sunnyside of Linden. We had a bunch of classes together in high school and got cool. He invited me to a bunch of parties over the time of our friendship and he always provided pills, weed, and whatever other drug the party goers wanted to get high on. All of my boys and the students at the college I was attending always got high on something and the white boy had everything they needed. Unfortunately, his connect got busted and the white boy never got back on his feet. Before long, AK and I bumped into a dude who could supply us with whatever we need, so I became the connect for the white boy. He takes a lot of our drugs and dispenses them to his white friends.

It was only right we linked with him because we have the supply and he knows the people to get our product to. From that point a great business union was formed. It's underhanded, but extremely lucrative and I deemed the risk to be worth the reward. AK has unimpeded access to street clientele and I have the university world on lock. Cash has been flowing ever since.

"Well shit, I'm about to bounce to class. Gotta beat the traffic. You know Bloomfield Ave. be crazy," I speak.

"Hell yeah.... I'm bout to go fuck wit old girl. She on some lunch at Menlo shit. Holla at me after you pick up the bread," AK speaks.

"That's what it is. Yo, we definitely at Velocity tonight though," I state.

I peace AK up and head to the whip. It's nice as hell out, so I drop the windows down and pop the sunroof open. Mob Deep just dropped Murda Muzik, so I have it blasting though my speakers. I know it's too loud for the city ordinance, but I have to listen to my music loudly. It's the only way I can feel the beat. The Quiet Storm Remix is my shit. I'm taking the local route to my university, so I can be seen and heard while I'm riding. I'm young, fresh, and have paper in my pocket. I'm good.

I'm driving up Bloomfield Ave. blasting my music when I see a cop tucked in the cut. Damn, I know 5-0 is going to fuck with me. I drive past the cop and as soon as I start thinking I'm in the clear, here his bitch ass comes. He pulls out of the spot he is tucked in and gets behind me. I know his duck ass is running my plates. There's no way he heard my music over all of the daytime traffic on Bloomfield Ave. The good thing is that I'm not worried. All of my paperwork is straight. Only a dumb ass would be hustling and have shaky paperwork.

I pull over as soon as I find a safe location. I know he's mad that it took me so long to pull over, but fuck him. Couldn't this bastard find a doughnut shop to hit up or something? I pull out my driver's license, registration and insurance cards in anticipation of him asking for them. I'm not trying to deal with this pig any longer than I have to. The cop stops behind me, jumps out of his car, and proceeds to my window.

"Good afternoon, young man," says the officer.

"Hi, officer," I reply.

"Do you know why I pulled you over today," he asks.

I answer, "No, I don't sir."

"Well, I pulled you over because your music was blasting very loudly. There's a city noise ordinance and you violated it. I could hear your music to the point I could actually hear the words," he states.

"Oh, I didn't recognize it as being that loud. I was in a zone just thinking about life. I have a lot going on in my personal life officer," I said.

"I understand that, but that doesn't mean you can violate the law. Let me get your license, insurance, and registration," he voices.

I hand him the paperwork and he goes back to the car. This cop better not make me late for class. I hate when the cops take twenty minutes to run my information knowing it doesn't take that long. They just do that to fuck with people and get them rattled, so they spaz out and give them a reason to lock the person up. I ain't beat though. I know the game and refuse to fall for their shenanigans. I look through the rear-view mirror and see another unit pull up. Damn, they're really going overboard for a music violation. These cops be bored as hell.

These fucking pigs are always bothering somebody. I'm just trying to go to college and get my education and they can't allow me to do that peacefully. You know what? I'm going to be an asshole to them today. Normally, I'm a peacemaker and very compliant when getting pulled over, but not today. They can't keep harassing me without any consequence. I won't do too much to them, but I will give them an earful. They won't have a reason to shoot me on the side of road.

The officer gets back out of the car and come to my window. The cop that was in the other patrol car gets out and walks along the passenger side of my vehicle. He is peering in my car as if he knows something that I don't. Oh shit! I forgot I have 3 ounces of weed in here. I guess I can't act like an asshole because if I do, they may want to search the car and would be justified. I guess I just have to make friendly with them.

The officer says, "You were blasting your radio pretty loudly there. I'm going to have to give you a citation for that violation. Where are you headed today? Do you have any weapons or drugs in the car with you today?"

"Sir I'm headed to Montclair State. I'm a student there. And no, I don't have any drugs or weapons on me officer," I reply.

"You're a student at Montclair State? What are you studying there?" the officer inquires.

"Yes, I'm in my second year at Montclair State and I'm majoring in English and minoring in education," I reply.

"That's pretty good. We need good teachers out there. That's a nice pair of sunglasses and pretty expensive-looking outfit you have on to be a college student," the cop states.

The other officer asks, "How are you able to afford such nice things on a college student's budget? Aren't most college students broke and struggling?"

"Yes sir, most college students do seem to be struggling, but I guess I'm just lucky. Also, I work in Newark Airport, so that helps pay the bills," I reply.

"You're a pretty good guy huh? Do you mind

if we search the car?" the officer asks.

"Yes, I would mind if you search the car. I really need to get to class and I don't want to be late. If you search the car, I'll be late for class for sure. Those professors up there are pretty strict about attendance and punctuality. They hate when students show up tardy for class. The look they give students when they come in late is enough to make the strongest man cry," I answer.

"I understand that you need to get to class, but I think I smell something coming from your trunk. And it doesn't seem like it's potpourri. And I'll be honest, something about you just doesn't sit right with me. You seem too calm to not have something going on," the officer responds.

I know the cop is lying. They really are the assholes that people make them out to be. He's really just saying he smells something so that way he can have a reason to search my vehicle. The bad thing is the weed is in the trunk.

I answer, "Everything is legit with me officer. I just work and go to school. No more, no less."

"Well, if that's the case, then you really shouldn't mind me just taking a quick peek through your car and letting you go about your business. You don't want us to have to call the dogs out and let them tell us what we think we know?" the officer questions.

Talk about being stuck between a rock and a hard place. I don't really want them to call the dogs out because the dogs will definitely smell the shit in the trunk. At the same time, I don't want to let them search the car either. What the fuck should I do? I hate these pig mother fuckers.

I decide the better of the two options is not to let them search the car. I'll take the chance that they're calling my bluff about the dog. The cops are taken aback after I don't give them permission to search the car.

However, one cop decides to walk around the perimeter of my car looking inside. He peers in the backseat and motions his partner over. His partner comes over and looks inside my car. They claim they see the handle of a gun and order me out of the car. I get out of the car at gun point. One officer goes to the backseat and pulls out my umbrella. They saw the handle and used that as an excuse to search my car. Next, he pulls the lever to lift the trunk and then walks to the back of the car and lifts the trunk up. The cop looks back at me and the other officer. After he sees the contents of my trunk, a devilish grin appears on his face.

"What's in the duffle bag?" he inquires as he looks in our direction.

"There's nothing but clothes in the duffle bag officer. I never know where I will end up from night to night, so I keep a fresh change of clothes in that duffle bag at all times," I verbalize.

"Do you expect me to believe that bullshit? Change of clothes you say huh? I guess you won't mind me searching it then?" he asks.

I answer, "I really don't like people looking at my personal belongings. I mean it's just some underwear, socks, and things like that in there. You really don't need to check it."

Both officers begin to laugh at my comment about my duffle bag. They find it funny that I actually don't like people rummaging through my stuff, especially personal belongings. Of course, the detective doesn't listen to my suggestion about not searching the bag.

"Well, buddy we have probable cause to search the car. Which means that we can search everything in the car so even though you don't want me to I'm going to search the bag," the officer states arrogantly.

This is some real-live bullshit. These cops have nothing better to do other than to try to wreck people's lives. But I'm not sweating it though. It's just typical BS that I have to deal with along with everything else. The cop rummages through my duffle bag and takes a step back when he catches the whiff of the contents of the bag.

"This is some strong shit you have in here. Talk about high powered. This is what I was smelling," the officer states.

The officer who is standing with me runs over to the trunk immediately. He gets to the trunk and reiterates what the other officer said. I have no idea what they are talking about. Wait! AK did have my whip! Ain't no telling what he may have left in the trunk. I'm fucked if he slipped up, but I didn't see shit back there. What the fuck! Next, they both start laughing.

What the hell is so funny? Wait a minute. I know what's so funny! They've checked my dirty clothes bag. I forgot that I have dirty basketball shorts and draws in the bag from when we played basketball at Saint Mark's Park. He must have searched that duffle bag in the trunk. I know by now that those shorts probably smell like death.

"Why didn't you warn us?" asks one of the officers jokingly.

I answer, "My bad fellas. I forgot that bag was in the trunk. I normally take it out immediately but I've been busy between school and work, so it slipped my mind."

The cops laugh so hard from rummaging through the bag with the funky clothes that they close the trunk and let me leave without even completing their search of my car. One of them even jokes that he's afraid to open the other bag because there may be more smelly clothes in it. I'm not complaining, I'm just ready to get out of here without any further delay. I get back in the car and head to class with only a ticket for violating the noise ordinance. That's a whole lot better than what it could have been. I could have went to jail for drug trafficking. Yeah, that would have been crazy.

# CHAPTER 3

I drive away and head to campus. I can't believe I was that damn close to getting pinched by the police. His ass really didn't have any reason to pull me over anyway. The pigs are always using some bullshit reason to pull niggas over. Oh well, I got away with it this time. They definitely would have locked my ass up and hit me with a distribution charge. Three ounces isn't much in Essex County, but you never know what will happen with asshole cops and prosecutors.

Those assholes give you more time in jail for selling weed then they do if you killed or molested somebody. That's the part of the law that I don't understand. I know they don't think a little bit of weed is worse than some kid's life being derailed. Shit, it's all about the money anyway. Everybody knows that we have a hypocritical ass government.

It makes me sick with the shit those cops come up with sometimes. He said he could smell the weed through the trunk and mistook and umbrella handle for a gun handle, but I know that was bullshit. I know he was lying because I have the weed in the trunk in a special compartment I had made when for I need to transport a little something. The compartment is vacuum-sealed, is airtight, and you can't smell anything inside of it. For some reason, this cop wants me to believe that he was able to smell it from the outside of the car with the trunk closed.

I know I have some high-grade shit but, it's not that good. He must have a dog's nose with superhuman powers on it. We all know that was just his excuse to get the dogs to come out or to allow him to search my car. They use that shit all the time, but I wasn't worried about it though.

The rest of the ride to campus is smooth sailing. I get up there with just enough time to get to my class on time. Class is cool and the time goes by quickly. Once class is over, I head straight to my boy's dorm, so I can drop these ounces off. I have to get this shit off of me before one of these punk ass campus cops tries to stop me too.

I have a high tolerance for nonsense and I'm very patient, but I think I might snap if another officer pulls me over with their nonsense. I get to my boy's dorm and call upstairs to let him know I'm here. He comes downstairs to sign me in and we head upstairs to his room to handle our business.

"Damn son, it seems like it's more bitches in this dorm every time I come through. You gotta put me down with something. I know one of your bitches got a homegirl or something that I can fuck wit," I comment.

"Nigga, you go to this school too. You better bag one of them bitches in your class. When I push up on the bitches it's just for me. You know how I do," Sean replies.

"That's what it is. I'm definitely gonna scoop one of these bitches on my own then. That bitch that checked me in is bad as hell!" I remark.

"She damn sure is. You should have said something to her. I know you wasn't scared," Sean jokes.

"Fuck out of here! You know damn well I ain't scared of nobody or nothing. You know I'm here on business, so I just ain't wanna be off point. Shit, I figured since this is your dorm that you could scream at her for me, but fuck it. I'll get at her," I explain.

Sean speaks, "I feel you. When I see her again, I got you. I think she be at the front counter all da time. I'll throw her your number or something."

"Hell yeah! That's what's up! Throw that skeezo my number. Shit, if she down there when I leave, I'll politic her myself," I say.

"True, and she don't really fuck wit nobody

like that. She keeps to herself mostly and I never see her out. Dat bitch fuck around and be wifey nigga," Sean utters.

"I don't know about all dat wifey shit. I'm just trying to hit that shit for now. Let me get dat money tho. I can't be up here fucking with you all night," I state.

I reach into my book bag and pull out the weed for Sean. Sean goes into his closet and pulls out a small scale. He wants to weigh the ounces to ensure that I'm not cheating him. I guess he doesn't trust me and I don't blame him because I don't trust him either. I mean we are cool as far as he buys shit from me, but I don't fuck with him like that outside of this business. He contacts me when his supply runs low and I get him straight.

He takes the first bag and lies it on the scale and of course it's the correct weight. He repeats the process with the other two ounces and gets the same result.

"Nigga, that shit straight. You didn't have to weigh all three. You know I don't fuck around when it comes to business. Square dealings is all I do," I assure.

"Man… listen. The last connect I had would count the weight of the zip lock bag as part of the weight of the ounce of weed, so you know I'm always gonna check. I know you don't do it like that, but I ain't trying to take an "L" for nobody," Sean narrates.

"I feel you. Niggas always be on their bullshit. Everybody trying to get over on everybody all the damn time. Dat shit ain't my style, but I feel you fam," I orate.

Sean hands me my money and I count it in front of him. While I'm counting the money one of Sean's boys comes into his room. I turn away from him immediately and walk towards the bathroom. I don't want to meet anyone I don't have to meet. The fewer the people who know what I do the better. Sean tells his boy to bounce and that he'll hit him up later. What asshole doesn't lock his door during a drug deal? He has to have more common sense than that. All of the money is here and I put it in my pocket. I peace Sean up and roll out. When I get downstairs, the girl is still at the counter, so I approach her.

"Excuse me, I gave you my ID when you checked me in earlier and now I don't have my ID," I say.

"I remember you and I remember giving you your ID back. All I did was write your name down and gave it right back. You must have lost it," she words.

"You remember me? What was so memorable that you remember me?" I ask.

"Yeah, I remember you because your cologne is banging," she answers.

"Good looking out ma! Your smile is banging too. My name is Rah," I voice.

"Boy, your name ain't no Rah. Your id said your name is Ray. Let me guess… Rah is what all of your boys call you. Everybody wants to be street. You too cute to be street," she verbalizes.

I say, "Yeah, my name is Ray and my boys nicknamed me Rah for a good reason."

"Rah and Ray are so close that you might as well stick with your real name. It's really the same thing," she speaks.

"You got a lot to say about names, don't you? Well, what's your name?" I inquire.

Unfortunately, the girl at the counter gets busy checking people into the dorm and is unable to answer my question. Damn, I know she's feeling me. A couple more minutes and I would have had her number for sure. I decide to chill for a few extra minutes to see if the line subsides, so I can resume my conversation with her.

I wait ten more minutes, but the girl's line isn't getting any shorter. It's actually getting longer with no end in sight, so I head to my car. There's no need to stick around any longer if she's going to be tied up. I get to my car and am slightly perturbed that I didn't get her number because I was really feeling her flow. Well at least I know where she works and can double back on her sometime in the future.

I take the Parkway back to Linden because I have to hit Sunnyside. Sunnyside is a section of Linden where all the white people live. There are a lot of houses that are well kept in this section of the city. More importantly for me is that I got a snow bunny over there who holds some of my shit. The good thing about taking the Parkway back to Linden is that the exit I need to take lets me off right in the back door of the Sunnyside.

There's no need to travel local streets when I'm doing dirt. I left campus a lot later than normal and missed all of the Parkway traffic. I get to my snow bunny's house in no time. This is perfect time for us to meet up because I am low on my shit and have mad niggas calling me for product.

I get to her house and pull into the garage. She's already waiting for me in the garage. We go inside and start heading for her room until I hear a female's voice. The voice I hear is that of her mother. She still lives with her parents and they are clueless as to what she does. Unfortunately, her mom is home, so I have to greet her.

Not that I'm antisocial or anything it's just that I don't like to talk to people if I don't have to. I briefly speak to her mom and then we proceed to her room, so I can re-up. Her room is like a mini loft. Her parents gave her the room over the garage and it's laid out. She has more space in this room than many people have in their apartments.

We chop it up about current events for a few minutes and then I let her suck me off. After I buss a crazy nut, I pack up some of my shit and head for the door. I don't know why she keeps all of this shit in here for me anyway. Shit, if the cops run up in this shit, it's a wrap for her and the entire family. I guess she isn't too worried about getting jammed up. When you live in the white neighborhood you can get away with murder.

We walk out of her room and head downstairs. I know her mom is going to think something is up because I came in empty handed and now I'm leaving with a bag. It would seem real suspect to me if I noticed someone go into a house with nothing and come out with a boatload of stuff. I thought I was going to have to sneak past her mom dukes with the shit, but I don't because she left while Samantha and I were making it do what it do.

I walk to the car and open the trunk. I stash the product in the stash spot I have built into the trunk. That's secure and undetectable, so I jump in the car. Samantha lets the garage door up and I back out. This time around I won't be pulled over. I can't afford to be pulled over with all the shit I have in the car with me. I make it back to my crib without incident. I unpack the product from the car and bring it in the crib with me. AK and I supply the dude who runs Velocity with the drugs he pumps out of the club, so I separate what I'm taking to the club and what I'm leaving here. I walk downstairs with a colorful laundry bag and throw it in the trunk. The laundry bag is to conceal what I'm really doing. If someone is watching me, they'll think I'm just organizing my laundry, but really, I'm tucking my product back in its proper location for transport. I've been on the move all day and now I'm going to chill for a little bit before we hit the club later.

As soon as I plop down on my bed, my side phone rings. It's in the living room on the charger and I really don't feel like getting up to answer it, but I do reluctantly. I see one of my peeps number flashing on the screen.

"Yo, what's good with you? You got some good news for me?" I ask as I answer.

Everything is good with me. I'm copasetic here. You know how I get down. Now you know I only call when I have good news," Gary says.

"That's what it is! I know how you get down. Fam, I'm just a cordial ass nigga and I know that respect always goes a long way in our business," I remark.

Gary shoots back, "That's real shit. Can't deny that."

Gary tells me that I should come to check him sometime real soon, so we agree on meeting time. I call AK immediately to let him know that we have a brand new power move to make soon.

# CHAPTER 4

AK and I decide to meet at the park before we hit Velocity. The park is our normal meeting location in most cases. AK always wants to be lifted before we go to the club, so we meet at the park. I drive to the park and see AK's car is already here. He's not sitting in his car, so I assume he's already on the bleachers.

I begin walking over to the bleachers when I hear AK calling me a slow bitch because he made it to the park before I did. He only beat me here because I had to make a quick stop. I don't respond to him and just proceed to the bleachers. AK has just finished rolling a blunt and begins to smoke it.

He takes a pull and begins to choke while he's inhaling. I start laughing because he's coughing like his lungs are about to come up. Additionally, he's pounding on his chest like he's King Kong or something.

"Damn nigga. You better catch that shit! Fuck around and choke to death," I joke.

AK is coughing so badly that he can't even say "fuck you" like he normally would when he chokes while blazing. However, AK does manage to muster enough composure to raise his middle finger at me. About ten seconds later he stops coughing.

"Fuck you bitch," he utters.

"Nigga, you can't smoke. What the fuck," I say.

AK replies, "Whatever nigga. Yo, it's gonna be mad bitches at Velocity tonight. I'm definitely fucking something."

"Hell yeah, it's gonna be crazy as hell. Nigga, you probably gonna be fucking Hanna Palm tonight," I shoot back.

"Nah, nigga that's you. You the whack off champion. Nigga beat off so much that you got your palm print on ya shit," AK cracks back.

"You got that, bitch!" I respond while I dap him up for getting his joke off.

This is normal interaction between me and AK. The jokes never stop going back and forth from the moment we get up until the time we part ways. The best part about it is if anybody else is with us the jokes are all one-sided. We go into attack mode on them. It's like that with everything; not just with jokes. If beef comes his way, then it also has to come my way and vice versa.

"Yo, but on some real shit though, we gotta drop that shit off at the club and then hit South Jersey after we leave Velocity. Ain't really gonna be no time to jump no bitches off," I inform.

"True. I forgot all about that shit. Well, if I spit the right shit, I'll fuck one of them bitches in da car on some other shit," AK voices.

"That's what's good," I comment.

AK finishes his "L" a few minutes later and we bounce. He jumps in the car with me since we have to take the drive after we leave the club and I already have the shit tucked in the hiding spot. We blast the new Mobb Deep CD the entire way there.

"Shit, I wanna smoke while we listen to this hot shit, but can't since we riding dirty," AK mentions.

"Man, that's ya thing, but you'd be dumb as hell to smoke another "L" with pounds of weed in the car," I verbalize.

"AK replies, "Word up. Would be setting ourselves up for the bullshit. I'm good though. That shit I just smoked was bonkers! I just wanna smoke to this album."

"No doubt. But you know they gonna play the "Quiet Storm" remix a hundred times in the club, so you can just smoke in there," I suggest.

"That's real!" AK speaks.

After a short drive, we arrive at Velocity. The parking lot is packed and the line is wrapped around the building. It doesn't matter that the parking lot is full because we are doing VIP parking. There's no way I'm parking where everyone else is parking with ten pounds of weed in the car. The dope thing is while we're in the club, the weed will be taken out of the car and the money will be dropped inside of it. We have it so good that we don't have to touch a thing.

We drive to the valet line and an attendant comes over to us. We jump out and walk to the building. The good thing about the valet here is that it's right by the front door. Nobody will be able to bother the whip without being detected. AK and I come here so much that we don't have to wait on that long ass line. We know most of the security team and the DJ.

We got cool with the staff because we always tip them and even send drinks to the DJ for doing his thing. Additionally, it doesn't hurt that AK is fucking one of the cocktail girls. We walk right into this spot like it's home just like Tony Montana walked straight into the Babylon Club in "Scarface".

I can't front, this is the life. We have people we don't even know showing us love and giving up props just because other people say we are worthy. We walk in and head straight to the DJ to peace him up. For the rest of the night, he'll be shouting us out over the mic.

"Yo, I saw two bad ass bitches on the line when we were walking in," I report.

"Word? Why didn't you bring them in with us? You think they still out there?" AK inquires.

"Cause I was just trying to get in here. Son, they gotta still be out there. They were towards the back of the line," I answer.

"True, I'm bout to go get them hoes," AK says.

I say, "You don't even know what they look like. Dig, one of them has on a yellow belly shirt with long hair. The other one is your complexion with some tight ass black jeans."

"Nah, nigga you coming to get them with me. Point them out when we get out there," AK orders.

We walk back outside to see if we see the two girls on line. I see them and point them out to AK. He, without hesitation, runs down on them.

"What's good ladies?" AK asks.

"Nothing, just tryin to get in da club," one of them answers.

"Word, well come on! You don't gotta wait on line. We'll walk you and your girl in," AK words.

"You serious?" one asks.

I nod my head in a yes motion and they jump off the line and follow us in. The two of them are curved in all the right areas and look good as hell. I point to the security guard as we walk back in and gesture to him that the two females are with us. He moves the rope for the VIP line and we breeze back in.

"Damn! Y'all doing it!" one of the girls states.

AK questions, "Yo, what you mean Miss?"

"I'm saying... Y'all came and got us off the line like y'all own this shit or something," she answers.

"Nah, we don't own this spot, but we be here though. They know us up in here heavy and we show love, so they show love in return," I say.

The other female responds, "I feel you. Y'all must be showing crazy love if y'all just walking in and out pulling people off the line like it ain't shit. Showing love must mean that y'all spending a lot of money in here. For real, for real."

"It could be because of that, but I ain't saying nothing. You'll have to decide for yourself why they show us love. Keep your eyes open for the night and tell us what you see," I voice.

"You want me to keep my eyes on you for the night, but I don't even know your name or your boy's name," she states.

I reply as I put my hand on her lower back and lean in close to her to whisper in her ear, "Damn, my bad ma, my name is Rah and my boy's name is AK. You look like your name should be Kim."

"Oh my goodness! That's crazy as hell! My name is Kim. I must really look like a Kim if you guessed it right just from a few minutes of talking to me," she responds excitedly.

"Get da fuck outta here! I ain't beat. Your name ain't no damn Kim. Let me see your id or something with your name on it," I order.

While she's opening her clutch to get her identification, I turn to AK and the other girl and ask what her friend's name is. She tells me to ask her friend and doesn't tell me. Finally, Kim has her id out of her clutch and hands it to me. I look at the name on the id and Kim starts laughing because her name really isn't Kim. Her name is actually Mya. She was just gassing me up like it was. I start laughing with her.

"Oh, so you got jokes, huh?" I ask.

"I guess. I figured since you wanted to throw names out there, I'd run with it. I had ya ass going for a few seconds though," Mya speaks.

AK is polying with the other girl whose name is Lisa. Me and Mya walk back over to them and we are all talking as a group. While we are talking, they tell us that they are from Sayreville, NJ. We tell them that we're from Jersey City, NJ. Of course, we are lying to them. We don't trust anybody enough to tell them our business and definitely not enough to tell some random broads in the club. We can't chance them running their mouths to somebody who may want to harm us. We all converse a little more and get some background information about each other.

"Aight! Enough of all this chitty chatty shit. I'm trying to party and get fucked up!" AK shouts.

"Word up! I'm feeling the partying, so let's go!" I say.

We start walking to the bar because AK has to

get a drink. He orders a Henny and coke like normal. I order my normal drink of a Sprite. I turn to Mya and Lisa and ask them what they want to drink. They both want a glass of Red Passion Alize.

"Talk about a girly drink! Alize ain't gonna get y'all no buzz," I joke.

AK turns to the bartender and says, "Give me a bottle of Red Passion Alize too."

"We like the way it tastes. We not trying to get fucked up and be in here falling all over the place drunk as hell," Mya says.

Lisa jumps in, "Yeah, you can speak for yourselves because Alize be having me buzzed. It's just enough to get me right."

Mya asks, "How you gonna shit on Alize and then order a whole bottle of it? You damn sure gonna drink some of it, right?"

"Hell no! I ain't drinking none of that bullshit. That bottle is for you and your girl," AK asserts.

"Nah, ma, he's not drinking any of it. He's serious as hell. It's too weak for him," I voice.

"Damn, I thought we are all gonna drink from it! That's a big ass bottle though," Mya speaks.

Lisa vocalizes, "That's the most expensive bottle of Alize they have. I guess we know where the money is. Well, pour me a glass because I'm trying to get my buzz on now!"

Mya thanks us and grabs her glass for me to pour her some Alize. All four of us walk over to the dance floor. However, we don't start dancing immediately. Instead, we post up on the outskirts of the dance floor while we drink and we talk as much as we can while the music is playing. Even though Mya and I have been talking more than AK and Lisa have been, we still don't know for sure which one of them is feeling me and which one is feeling AK.

Me and AK decide not to push up on either one of them because we don't want to mess up our chances of bagging them. If he hollers at the one who likes me and not the one who is big on him, we'll potentially not get either one of them. We have to do something that will make it obvious who is feeling who. In order to find out who is feeling who, I signal the DJ to play me and AK's theme song.

The DJ knows what track we want to hear because we've done this before. While a song is playing, the DJ mixes in a snippet of the beat of the "Quiet Storm Remix". When the crowd hears the beat, they erupt with a cheer. AK gives me that look as if it's about to go down. We love the way the DJ entices the crowd by subtly dropping the beat to our track. Seconds later, he drops the track fully. The crowd is going wild and AK and me head straight to the center of the floor. We rock to the track as the DJ shouts us out.

The DJ plays the track about halfway through and restarts the track. The crowd's energy level jumps one hundred notches. It's almost like the club goers are infused with a hit of adrenaline directly to their veins. AK and I are no different than the other club goers. We are more hyped up than they are. We look in the direction of Mya and Lisa and motion them over to us. We'll know who is feeling who by whom they come to dance with. Mya comes over to me and starts dancing in my face and Lisa two steps in front of AK. We now know who is interested in who. To get things rolling a little faster and spice things up, AK gives the DJ another signal for when to end the song.

Moments later "Back That Thang Up" begins blaring across the club. This song is really a girl's song, but we always get the DJ to play it when we are dancing with girls. We know as soon as the beat drops that females will start grinding their asses on us and that's what we desire. This will give us an opportunity to grab on them without it being a problem. Mya is throwing her ass back on me like her life depends on it. I can't even front like her ass isn't soft and fat as hell.

AK is getting served just as lovely as I am. Lisa is bent over with her hands on the floor and is busting her ass back on AK like her ass is a hammer and his crotch is a nail. AK is all smiles and gives me the head nod of approval. We keep dancing throughout the song. Mya and Lisa stop bouncing their asses on us and face us respectively. We're now facing each other and still dancing. AK stays true to form and picks

Lisa up in mid-air. She is riding him as he grips her ass and she rubs his head. Meanwhile, Mya is popping her pussy on me while we continue dancing to the track.

Finally, the song ends and AK lets Lisa down and we all exit the dance floor. Mya and Lisa tell us they are going to the bathroom to get right. AK and I go back to the bar, so he can get another drink. AK orders his drink and we converse for a minute.

"This shit is bananas, son," I exclaim.

"Hell yeah. Son, I think these bitches are ready too," AK words.

"Ain't no question. Yo, we definitely can fuck tonight," I assert.

"Shit, we gotta go get the shit though. Nigga, we can't let these bitches get away without fucking them. I had Lisa in the air riding my shit. Yo! Son, I gotta fuck her tonight," AK utters.

I reply, "We just gotta see what it's looking like. My nigga, I'll fuck the shit outta Mya. She was grabbing my dick while we were dancing. Talking bout damn, I'm holding. I'm saying to myself I know bitch."

"Word up. I'll bust Lisa's ass too. We gotta see if they trying to fuck. For real. We can work something out with picking the shit up," AK says.

Lisa and Mya return from the bathroom and we continue right where we left off. We all party as if this is our last night on earth. The DJ continues to play hit after hit and shouts us out.

The club will be closing in another hour and it doesn't make sense for us to stay here until it closes because we're trying to bone these chicks and we still have to take this drive. I figure we'll be better off if we take the chicks to a hotel and do what we do then we can get on the road. I inform AK of what I think we should do and he agrees. I'm not surprised because he's always down for whatever.

AK says as he turns to Lisa and Mya, "We're about to bounce outta here."

"Say word! Velocity doesn't close for another hour, so y'all should close it out with us. It's too early to leave," Mya states in a disappointed tone.

I reply, "Yeah, we know they aren't shutting it down for another hour or so, but we have some moves to make. We gotta get outta here."

Lisa chimes in, "Hold up! It's the middle of the night and you two have to make a move. I guess we know what you two do for a living. It makes sense now the way you were spending a bunch of money all night."

"I don't know what you're talking about. We have to pick our homeboy up from the airport in Atlantic City. His flight comes in mad early, so we gotta get down there. Look at you assuming the worst," AK explains while lying through his teeth.

I can tell from the looks on their faces that they only slightly believe AK's bullshit story. We don't care if they buy the story or not. We just know that we'll never come clean as to why we're going to make a move in the middle of the night. We just met these chicks, so there's no way that they can know what we do. I might as well stop beating around the bush and see if we can hit tonight.

"Since you acting like you don't want the night to end, you and your girl should come back to the hotel with us, so we can chill some more," I say to Mya exclusively.

"That could work. I'm down with that, but I go where my girl goes. If she's not down, then we'll just have to get up another time," Mya explains.

I tell Mya that I understand that she won't leave her girl. I also tell her to find out what her girl wants to do. There's no reason to waste any more time in here if her friend is down to get a room. Mya goes to talk to Lisa to see what's good and AK and I converse. After about five minutes of talking, Mya returns with the verdict.

"We'll get a room with y'all, but we not leaving. We're spending the night and will stay until it's checkout time. Ain't no way we getting put out like some jumps in the middle of the night," Mya states.

AK replies, "That's cool. The room is yours to stay until checkout. We wouldn't put y'all out like that. We better than that. Don't forget that we have to make a move at some point, so we'll be leaving out."

"That's cool. We didn't forget that you have to go to the airport or wherever you claim you have to go. We'll just stick with the airport story," remarks Lisa sarcastically.

We leave the club immediately and head for a hotel. AK and I have standards, so we won't just stay anywhere. We have the girls following us as we drive down route 22 west until we find a hotel that's to our standards. AK jumps out of the car and goes to see if they have any rooms available. I get out of my car and keep Mya and Lisa company for a few minutes. Finally, AK returns and flashes me the room key. We're good to go and the games are about to begin.

We all make small talk as we head to the room. We get to the room and Mya sprawls across one of the beds as soon as we enter. Lisa beelines for the other bed and stretches across it as well. AK turns on the TV and I sit in the office chair. We don't have all night for small talk, so we have to handle our business now.

I state, "Mya, you should let me give you a back rub. You look a little tense and I can help loosen you up."

She asks, "Is that right? How do I look that I need a back rub? What about me says that I'm tense?"

"I just know these things. I'm nice like that and you know you need one, so stop fronting and playing hard to get," I respond.

"Whatever, I can't even lie. A massage doesn't

sound bad at all. You better be able to give a good massage. I'm a little concerned about your back-massaging skills because your hands look weak," Mya shoots back at me.

"That's what's good. You'll see my skills in a little bit. Trust me baby girl, I'm nice with mine. I promise you that," I shoot back.

"Okay, I guess I'm about to find out," states Mya as she flattens herself out on the bed, so I can begin massaging her back.

AK states, "Yo, she thinks that you're gonna massage her back right now like that. She doesn't know what a real back massage is, son."

"I know son. She has no idea of what a real back massage is. You can tell. Look at her, yo," I return in agreement.

"Umm, I know what y'all not gonna do! You not gonna play my girl out, so chill. She knows that she can get a better massage with her shirt off, but she doesn't want to take it off yet," Lisa jumps in to defend Mya.

"Thanks girl. They think they are on it, but they aren't. We got this and I was waiting for you to take my shirt off because you were the one talking about a massage. Handle your business," Mya comments sharply.

"You still don't get it. I'll have to show you how I give massages. I give spa-like massages. Ain't nothing normal about how we get down," I state.

I walk over to the bed and take Mya's shirt off.

Her titties are juicy and perky. I can tell she doesn't need a brazier to hold them up. My dick slightly stiffens as I look at her in her laced bra. AK flips through the TV channels and stops on the pay-per-view channel. He orders a porno movie and begins watching it. Lisa is fully attentive to the porno as well. I reach behind Mya and unclasp her bra. Her boobs are fully exposed and I rub her light brown nipples.

The porno is playing and we're all watching it. Mya and Lisa are paying close attention to the movie. I continue rubbing Mya's titties. She moans sensually as do I.

Lisa blurts out, "What the fuck is he doing?"

"Girl, I was thinking the same damn thing. He ain't even eating her damn pussy right! Like what the fuck!" Mya speaks in an aggravated tone.

AK voices, "Shit, you said that like you can eat pussy better than him or something!"

I dap AK up, as I say, "Right, my nigga. You reading my mind!"

Lisa sucks her teeth and states sternly, "Damn right, I said it like that cause I eat pussy better than him on the flick and probably better than you and your homeboy."

Mya says enthusiastically, "Let these niggas know. AK ass was trying to play you!"

I chime in sarcastically, "Well the way I see it is that it's only one way to tell who eats pussy better in this room and that's to have a competition."

Lisa remarks, "You ain't said nothing, but a

word. Y'all niggas must not know who you fucking with tonight. We ain't no basic bitches."

Lisa gets off the bed she's on and comes over to the bed that me and Mya are on. Lisa motions me out of the way and tells Mya to lie flat on her back. Mya complies with Lisa's instruction. I stand up and watch to see what's going to happen. AK watches on as well. Lisa kisses Mya sensually and Mya returns the advances. Lisa gropes Mya's juicy ass as she licks down her neck. Lisa starts sucking Mya's titties. Mya moans in euphoria.

AK yells out, "Yo, just cause you sucking her titties don't mean you gonna eat her pussy. She pump faking!"

I respond, "Hell yeah, she ain't bout dat action!"

Lisa stops licking Mya's titties and comments harshly, "Fuck both of y'all. All you two are doing is standing and watching. At least I'm goin in!"

AK shoots back, "Well, if what you're doing is goin in, we're in for a long and boring ass night. Fuck is you talking about?"

"Whatever nigga! Take ya shit off then," Mya vocalizes.

I, without hesitation or verbal response begin taking my clothes off. Lisa takes her pants off and is wearing a thong. Lisa pulls down Mya's leggings and exposes Mya's pussy. Mya isn't wearing any panties. Lisa wastes no time cloaking

Mya's pussy with her mouth. Lisa licks all around Mya's pussy and then gently fan blades her tongue on Mya's clit. Mya moans in stupefaction.

"Damn, she really eatin the fuck outta her pussy! She wild as hell!" AK asserts.

"I didn't think she had it in her," I say as I take off the rest of my shit.

Lisa is fingering Mya's ass as she eats her pussy. AK strips down butt naked also. I didn't get naked for nothing, so I walk over to the bed and start kissing Mya while Lisa is eating her out. My dick is rock hard and I'm ready to fuck. I stop kissing Mya and put my dick on her lips. She kisses the head of my dick softly three times. Mya grabs my dick and wraps her mouth around it.

She sucks my dick masterfully. She gags on it. Mya takes my dick out of her mouth and spits on my dick and starts sucking it again. I grab her by one of her shoulders and pump her face slowly. Lisa is bent over on the bed with her ass tooted in the air. AK grabs the string of Lisa's thong and pulls it to the side. He inserts his dick inside her and strokes her pussy as she eats Mya out.

"Damn, ma! Ya head is fire! Ooh, I like this shit! Hell yeah!" I say as I grip the back of Mya's head.

"Da fuck, this pussy wet as shit!" AK shouts out.

"I know it is nigga. And it's tight as hell!" Lisa states as she stops eating Mya out.

AK starts pumping Lisa harder and harder. Lisa is screaming as she looks back at AK in amazement. Lisa's ass is clapping on AK's dick as he fucks her out of control.

"Harder dammit! Harder dammit!" Lisa yells as she smacks her own ass.

AK pulls Lisa closer to the end of the bed. He plants his feet firmly on the floor. Lisa arches her back and buries her face in the mattress. AK goes back to pounding Lisa from the back.

"How you want it?" I ask Mya.

"I want that big ass dick hard and fast!" Mya answers.

I respond, "Flip your ass over then, so I can fuck the shit outta you! I want ya shit doggie."

"We gonna see about that," Mya remarks.

Mya grabs a pillow and flips over. She is bent over in the doggie style position. Her ass is juicy and unblemished. There is a straight shot to the pussy. She doesn't have any extra fat blocking the path to her pussy. I beat my dick on her ass. I stick my dick in her pussy and begin stroking her slowly. Mya moans louder and louder. I take my dick out of her pussy and rub her clit with it.

"What the fuck is you doing right now? I want you to fuck me. I ain't here to make love nigga. Pound my shit like you hate me that's the only way I can cum!" Mya informs frankly.

I grab Mya by the hips as I stand up and ram my dick back in her. I pound her wet pussy over and over as she screams my name. All that can be heard in the room is moaning, grunting, and the sound of asses being clapped on.

"Yo, it sound like that pussy is good as hell over there!" I yell over to AK.

"Hell, yeah my nigga. It's definitely fire!" AK assures.

"I'm bout to get some of that!" I voice.

AK yells out, "Switch!"

AK stops fucking Lisa and I stop fucking Mya. He walks over to where Mya is bent over at and begins fucking her. I walk over to Lisa and stick my dick in her. She sighs deeply as she feels the girth of my dick. Her body tenses up.

"Shit, don't tense up now. All that shit you was talking earlier bout to come back to bite you!" I word confidently.

"I ain't no lil ass girl nigga. Let's get there!" Lisa boasts.

"That's what the fuck it is!" I vocalize excitedly.

I pound Lisa repeatedly as she screams and tries to run from the power and weight of my dick, but I have her locked in. She can't run or hide. Lisa takes the sheet and stuffs it in her mouth and bites down on it. That's all she can do to cope with the combination of pain and pleasure. AK is waxing Mya's ass too. She's over there loving it.

# CHAPTER 5

"Yo, AK! Wake your ass up! We gotta roll asap!" I voice forcefully.

AK rolls over and looks at his phone. He immediately jumps up and starts putting on his clothes. Mya and Lisa are both still knocked out. AK goes into the bathroom and cleans up. He comes out of the bathroom and we bounce.

AK and I jump in the car and get on the highway. We listen to music as we drive. We're on top of the world. We're young, healthy, looking good, and feeling good. The best part about it is that we have a bunch of paper to play with. It seems like wherever we go we always have a happy ending. It's the life we deserve and it's the life we have created for ourselves.

"Yo, we bust those bitches' asses!" AK boasts proudly.

I respond excitedly, "Nigga, hell yeah we did!

That shit was epic!"

"Nigga, I almost passed out when that broad started crying while I was fucking her. Talking about the dick is too good," AK comments.

I say, "Son, the whole night was a movie! We balled out at the club and then got some new pussy and we switched off on them hoes. That shit was bananas!"

AK voices, "Yeah fam, that was definitely what it was. Last night is up there for best ever hands down."

AK and I stop talking and listen to music. Not that we don't have plenty to discuss because we do. However, our silence is more about being focused. We never even plan it to go this way, but somehow it always does. Subconsciously, we know we need to focus. The thing with the drug game is that you have to be focused at all times because if you're not, things will go awry quickly. One wrong move can have you sitting in a box for years or potentially even dead.

One thing I've learned during my years in the game is that it's heartless. No one has sympathy for you in the game. You can get shot and the game will go on without you. It stops for no one. You can be the man on the streets one minute and the next minute you can be forgotten about. The drug game and the street life are both highly competitive. That's why you have to be cutting edge when it comes to all of your moves. You have to be sharper than a Ginsu knife because there's always someone looking to take your spot. Not to mention, the police are always trying to build a case to throw you in jail.

One thing I know is that AK and I are not going down in a hail of gunfire from some young boy who's trying to get clout off of killing us and we're not trying to do no bids either. The plan is to get up enough money to be able to bounce out the hood. We're going to leave this place and never return. Fortunately, we're getting close to our goal. All of this moving and shaking will be a thing of the past. I'm heading to one of the southern states and will buy a house and just chill. I'll be way ahead of the game.

You see, I never wanted to use the drug game to be a way of life. I only want to use it to get up enough capital to bounce. I know this lucrative system can progress me years ahead and it's all coming together. Another year of this life and I'm out of Jersey for good.

"Yo, stop at the next exit so we can get some snacks," AK says.

I state, "Hell no! You know I don't make any stops until we get to the town we're going to. You'll be good on the snacks until we get there."

"Man, you and your bullshit superstitions. Ain't shit gonna go wrong because we stop. Nigga, you bugging," AK remarks.

I verbalize, "Wait. Wait. You know it's not bullshit because the two times I've been driving and we stopped for a snack there's always been drama."

"Fuck all that. I'm just trying to get some snacks," AK replies curtly.

I word, "That's what I thought. You know both times I stopped the load got fucked up or the driver got jammed up. Fam, I ain't stopping.

"I feel you with ya scary ass," AK jokes.

"Wake me up when we get there. I'm bout to steal like thirty minutes," AK utters as he yawns.

"Ole sleepy ass nigga," I clown.

AK puts the seat back, covers his face with his hat, and falls asleep. I turn the radio up and just vibe while we ride. Some people get mad when people go to sleep while they drive, but not me. It doesn't bother me one bit. It just gives me more time to think about some of everything. I could easily think of a new way to move our product or think of a new way to flip some bread. Either way, I'm good.

We finally make it to Cherry Hill. I see we need gas and AK wanted to stop, so I pull into a gas station on Fulton Street. I tap AK to wake him up. He isn't moving the fastest, but he's coming to consciousness. The gas station attendant knocks on the glass. He just pissed AK off in doing so. I roll the window down.

"Yo, what the fuck man? Why the fuck you knocking on the damn window so hard?" AK asks angrily.

The attendant replies, "I'm sorry my friend. It was not on purpose."

AK replies, "I bet the fuck it wasn't!"

I chime in, "Man don't knock so damn hard again and fill the tank up."

The attendant begins to fill the tank up. AK is yawning and getting ready to go inside the convenience store connected to the gas station. I look through the window of the store towards the register. I immediately jump out the car and run inside the gas station because I recognize the girl at the counter.

"Yo, what's good? Don't I know you from somewhere?" I ask.

"Umm, if you knew me, you wouldn't have to ask me that. I'm just saying," the girl behind the counter says sharply.

"Ouch, I see you have a slick tongue no matter where you are," I shoot back.

The girl replies frankly, "No, I just speak my mind wherever I'm at."

"Word. I ain't mad at that," I reply. "I see you have a thing for working counters."

"Umm, do I know you? And are you gonna buy something?" she asks.

I can't even front like I'm not shocked that she doesn't remember me. This is the first time I've ever met a girl and she not remember me later. I don't know if that means she wasn't feeling me or if it means she is just not impressed by the flash. Who the hell knows!

"Yeah, I know you. You're a fellow Red Hawk. I met you at your other job when you were working the counter," I tell.

"Oh, you go to Montclair State too. That's what it is! I meet like a thousand people a day at that counter and hundreds more at this one. I forget all those faces. For real. For real," she explains. "But you don't know me if you only saw me at the counter."

"Yeah, I go there, but I don't live on campus. I got my own spot. Well, me and my boy stay together. My name is Ray," I vocalize. "I guess 'know' is improper."

She speaks, "Improper... well, it's really inaccurate. The word "know" means more than you just saw me at a counter. Wait, you said Ray. You're the guy who had on the sunglasses and was holding up my counter. Don't you have like two first names? Ray and Run or something."

"You're right. I don't know you, but I spoke to you. And yes, it's Ray and Rah. I'm sure you have a name," I say.

AK walks in the store. The girl greets him and he speaks back. AK goes to the fridge and grabs a Snapple and some chips.

"Yo, do you want something?" AK asks me.

I answer, "Yeah, get me a mango Snapple and some cookies."

"For sure," AK replies.

I turn to the girl at the counter and resume our conversation. AK walks over to the counter and puts our items on it. The girl grabs the items and rings them up.

"So, do you have a name?" I ask.

"Of course, I do. That's a silly question for you to ask," she articulates.

"I'm saying, what is it?" I ask.

"It is eight dollars and thirty-seven cents. Will that be cash or charge?" she answers.

AK walks away from the counter and starts to exit the store. Confusedly, I look over at him. He seems like he's perturbed at something. I have to see what's up with him because he was just fine.

"Yo, you good?" I inquire.

"Yeah, I'm good. I left my cash in the car. That's it, I'm bout to go get it," AK answers.

AK walks out the store. I go in my pocket and pull out a wad of money. I have nothing smaller than fifty-dollar bills in this wad. I grabbed the money out of this pocket on purpose because I want to impress the girl behind the counter. I peel a fifty off and hand it to her.

"You funny as hell! You know when I asked what is it, I wasn't talking about the total. I was talking about your name," I state.

As she grabs the fifty, she speaks, "Well, how you know I want you to know my name? You could be a stalker or something."

"I'm no stalker. I'm just trying to make a connection with you and knowing your name would be a good start," I verbalize.

She hands me my change and replies, "You can get that. My name is Dionna."

"Word, it's nice to finally know your name and

be able to put it with such an angelic face," I compliment.

"Thank you," Dionna voices.

"You got it. Yo, let me get your number, so I can hit you up."

"I'm gonna have to say no because I don't know you to give you my number," Dionna utters.

AK opens the door and peaks his head inside. He taps his wrist as if there's a watch on it. I know it's time for us to roll, but I don't want to. I really want to send AK to handle the business and I stay here with Dionna. I'm disappointed that she won't give me her number, but it is what it is. I respect that she won't give it to me. I really am still a stranger to her.

"I can respect your decision. Dionna, I hope to see you on campus or something," I orate.

"That'll be cool. See you around Ray," Dionna voices.

I walk away from the counter holding the bag of snacks. I can't let it go down like this. I need to make a gesture that may make her remember me. Hmm, what can I do? I quickly look around the store to see if something catches my eye. Fortunately, something does catch my eye. There is a bin with single stem roses in it. I walk over to the bin and grab one. I pull five dollars out of my pocket and pay for it.

"Dionna, this is for you. I hope you remember me next time. Enjoy your shift. I'm out," I word.

Dionna surprises me with her response to my flower. I've only talked to her twice, but I can already tell that she speaks her mind and doesn't bite her tongue. She's clearly very witty. I can tell that because for her to respond the way she does to my questions and answers she has to have some intellect. I also can tell that she's hard to impress and is not the type of woman to hang on every word a man says. Before I walk out the door, she calls my name, so I stop in my tracks and turn around.

"Hey, this flower is kinda sweet of you. I basically just rejected you and you still thought to buy me a rose. That was very sweet and a first for sure. Most dudes curse me out when I don't give them my number," Dionna explains warmly.

I say, "The good thing about me is that I'm eons away from being most dudes. Any dude who would curse a woman out for not submitting to his desires is merely a boy."

"You can say that again. Well listen, I know you gotta go, but you should take my number down and hit me up some time," Dionna voices.

I respond happily, "Yeah, I do gotta roll and I'd like that a lot."

Dionna tears a piece of paper from the paper receipt roll and writes her number on it. She hands it to me and I feel like I've just won a first-place ribbon. I've never been so excited about getting a girl's number in my life. This is an unusual feeling for me. I'm surprised I didn't rip her arm out of its socket when I took the number from her.

"FYI, money doesn't make me jump through hoops. That little charade you and your boy pulled was corny to me. It was totally unnecessary. In my eyes, it did more harm than good," Dionna offers directly.

I figure she's talking about AK coming in the store and then I whip out a wad of cash. The funny thing is that wasn't a cabal we put together to get me closer to her. That's just how me and AK get down. Sometimes he pays and other times I do. It's just love and money means nothing between us. Besides that, I always have a bunch of cash on me. This front pocket money is a drop in the bucket for me. I decide not to tell Dionna that we didn't choreograph anything because it's not worth it. Instead, I play it cool.

"I feel you. That's good to know. I can see how it's a bad look," I respond.

I walk out the door and head to the whip. I'm hyped up to say the least. I sit in the car and look at the paper she wrote her number on. I start memorizing her number immediately. I save the number in my phone too, but I'm not risking only having Dionna's number stored in one place.

"Yo, you good? You staring at that number like it's about to disappear or some shit," AK comments.

I remark, "Shit, you never know. That's why

I'm memorizing it right now. Fam, I'm not losing her number."

"Ole girl at the counter gave you her number? I'm surprised as hell. The way she was talking I just knew she wasn't fucking with you on that number shit. That's what it is. That bitch bad as hell!" AK articulates.

"Yeah, yo she slid me her digits. She wasn't wit it at first then she threw it to me. I had to work for it, but I got it though," I convey. "On some crazy shit, I met her at Montclair State. She go there too."

"Say word! What the fuck she doing down here then? We far as hell from Montclair my nigga," AK states.

"I don't know and didn't even get a chance to ask. Maybe she down here for the same reason we down here," I reply jokingly.

"If she is, that's my kinda bitch!" AK shoots back. "Nah, but for real, she gotta live down here. Ain't no way she down here working and don't live around here somewhere."

"That's the same thing I was thinking. Chick ain't working down here if she ain't from here," I voice.

"Either way, you'll find out very soon after you bust her ass. Just like all these other bitches," AK tells.

I comment, "I got a feeling that's this one's different, but I'll see soon."

"Yo, that's good. Real good. Peep this, nigga,

you know how coincidences work," AK comments.

I reply, "Nigga, I'm way ahead of you. I'm gonna find out if Gary is her peeps ASAP."

"True, I should've known you were already on it," AK comments.

I voice, "You already know my nigga. I don't miss a beat."

"Aight, let's make it. We got to get outta here," says AK.

I put the car in drive and we roll out. We only have a few more minutes to our drive. The person we're meeting lives a couple miles away. Of all the times we've been down here, we've never stopped at that gas station, but I sure am glad we did today. I still can't believe old girl was in there. Out of all the places in Jersey to bump into her, we meet again in Cherry Hill.

"Yo, call old boy and let him know we're on his block," I say.

AK pulls out his cell phone and calls Gary. Gary is our connect who lives in Cherry Hill. He gives us the best prices for weed and the birds, so we always deal with him. The last connect we had for product started to raise his prices too much, so we had to look elsewhere. It was a business move, so there were no hard feelings. We just moved on. It's the nature of the game. If you want to make it in this game, you have to be willing to monitor and adjust.

AK calls Gary and tells him to pop the garage

door. We pull directly into his garage and the garage door shuts behind us. Gary is standing in the garage with two duffle bags unzipped. As always, Gary has a nine-millimeter pistol in his hand. Out of all the times we've come to get the dope, he's always had his pistol in his hand. It's definitely locked and loaded. Shit, I don't blame him either. There are way too many people out here jacking each other for product, so it's in his best interest to protect himself. If not, he could end up being the next person left stinking somewhere.

AK and I aren't into robbing anyone for their stuff. We're just two dudes from Linden, New Jersey looking to come up. Most people would be offended, but we're not because we know it's only business. Our dealings with Gary are only business and will be treated as such. He's not our friend and we're not his friends.

"G, what up man? How you?" AK inquires.

"Shit, normal biz. You know how the shit go," Gary answers.

"No doubt. I damn sure do. Ain't shit on our end either. Just trying to handle this right here and get out back up the way with no drama," AK voices.

"I feel you," Gary words.

"Now that you two are all caught up let's get to this business," I state.

Gary responds, "I ain't mad at cha. Let's handle our handle."

AK approaches the bags and asks, "What we looking like?"

Gary answers, "It's what we discussed. One bag with five birds and the other bag got seventy-five pounds of that good green shit. I smoked that shit myself and it's bananas! Some high-grade shit for real."

"That's what's up! I'm assuming the china white is of the same quality," AK verbalizes.

Gary comments, "You know how I roll. It's the best in the streets."

"Nigga, I don't know about all that. He hyping his shit up," I joke. "Well, I hope it is what you say it is."

"Damn right it is!" Gary boasts.

AK goes to the trunk of our car and pulls out a scale. He brings it over to the table where the product is sitting and begins to weigh it. He weighs each pound of weed individually. AK gives me the thumbs up after he weighs each pound to let me know the weights are right. AK passes me the scale and I weigh the kilos. After I weigh each one, I give AK the thumbs up.

"G, looks like everything is a go," AK speaks.

"Like always. You know I take this shit serious just like you do," Gary offers.

"Hell yeah. That's why we fuck with you," AK utters.

I go to the trunk of our car and pull out two gym bags. I walk back over to the table where the drugs are and put them in the empty bags we brought with us. We tuck the bags in the trunk of the car where the spare tire is supposed to go. We peace Gary up and we roll out. We're in and out of Gary's garage quickly just like normal.

We drive past the gas station where Dionna is working, but we don't stop. I can't even front like I don't want to stop to chop it up with her again, but I know now is not the time. We have a trunk load of shit that we need to get out the car immediately. AK and I get all of the product on consignment. We work so well together that we never have any issues on paying what we owe. We know what can happen if we don't pay in full or on time, so we always make sure we pay Gary his money back first.

AK and I go back and forth about just paying for the product on the front end, so we'll own it outright, but we never do. We like the idea of getting it for free on the front end even though we know it's not free. It's really just a mind thing. We just left Gary's crib with several kilos of cocaine and multiple pounds of weed without paying a dime. It's like robbing with no gun. Meeting Gary is the easy part, but this drive back to the stash house is always the difficult part.

Anything can go wrong on the drive back to north Jersey. We're like sitting ducks in this car. If the police were to pull us over, we'd be fucked for life if they searched the car. The crazy thing is that AK and I are less worried about the police and more worried about getting jacked for the load. That's the only reason we ride together on these runs. We're definitely on our Ps and Qs. We're not speeding, our signal lights work, and we have on our seatbelts.

"Man, we basically got this shit sold already. You know the weed is gonna disappear as soon as we touch back and the coke is gonna fly too. The white boy I'm cool with wants three of the keys and he's gonna pay for them outright," I orate.

AK states, "I love this shit! It's too easy. We'll send Gary his money for the shit in a few days from the way it sounds and the rest is all us. We'll be going back to him to re-up soon."

I reply, "This shit is too easy for real. We got a good system and we gotta stick to it."

The drive seems long like it always does when we're riding dirty, but it's just about over. We make it to the stash house and put most of the shit inside. We have people who are waiting for us to drop them what they want to purchase, so we hit them up. I call the white boy to let him know I'm on the way. I want to get rid of this shit as soon as possible. There's no need to hold on to three keys if I don't have to. AK calls some of his people who are looking to get some work from him too.

"Yo, be safe out there. Get at me later," AK says.

"Most definitely. I'll holla at you later," I reply.

AK and I depart, so we can handle our

business.

# CHAPTER 6

AK and I are coming off lovely. The best move we've ever made was getting off the corners to sell drugs. It was just too much work and was definitely too much risk. Our transition to selling weight is much more profitable and the chances of getting caught are drastically reduced. The game is also very violent and being on the streets selling drugs is a volatile situation. Shootouts and fights over drug turf are normal occurrences. Thankfully, selling weight has been different.

AK and I only deal with the people we know and that makes things far more predictable than the streets. Even though it's safer, AK and I know that there are risks associated with selling weight. We could easily get jacked by one of the people we sell weight to. For this reason, AK and I always keep our head on a swivel. Not to mention, we could walk into our connect's spot to re-up and be met by a thousand cops, but it's the nature of the game. These are some risks to the lives we live and we accept them wholeheartedly.

It's been a few months since I got Dionna's number at the gas station. Dionna and I are inseparable for the most part. Outside of my side business, work, and school we're always on the move. It doesn't matter what we do as long as we're chilling. AK and I aren't even hanging as much as we used to. He jokes all the time with me about leaving him hanging. I ain't sweating it because he knows it's all love. He's not mistaken though. I have dipped on him several times so me and Dionna could chill. I have to admit that I'm a bit different since I met her. I'm not even hollering at any other females right now.

I pull up to campus and walk over to class. English Literature is one of my favorite classes. I've always been good with grammar and writing, so I've always found these types of classes to be fun and easy. There are a bunch of females in this class who have been trying to holler at me, but I've been dissing them. I only have eyes for one woman right now. My nose is open wider than the Holland Tunnel. I'm heading to the cafeteria right after class to meet D and I can't wait.

"Alright, be sure to read the next two chapters in your textbook. Then answer the discussion questions at the end of the chapters," Professor

James instructs.

I ask, "Do we need to submit the answers online or bring them to class?"

Professor James answers, "Bring your answers to class and be ready to discuss them, but you must have a hard copy to turn in. If there are no more questions, you are dismissed."

I pack my belongings and roll out. I walk over to the cafeteria to meet Dionna. I walk in the cafeteria and see Dionna sitting in the corner of the cafeteria. She's always in the corner in her favorite booth. She has her back to me and is bopping her head to some music she's listening to. I ease up behind her and pull one side of her headphones out.

"What's good?" I ask as I sit down beside her.

Dionna replies, "Nothing, just reading this article for class."

I speak jokingly, "Seems like you were practicing breaking your neck listening to your music. I thought your neck was gonna break."

Dionna chuckles, "Whatever, you got jokes. I wasn't even going that hard. You wilding right now."

"Yeah, aight. You know your neck hurts. Let me give you a neck massage," I shoot back as I attempt to grope her neck.

"Boy, whatever," Dionna says as she pulls away from me playfully.

This is our relationship. It's a relationship of all jokes and mutual respect. There no beef or bullshit between us. We have a great time together and don't worry about what the outside world thinks about us. It's our relationship to grow or ground, so we're not pressed for outside opinions or influences. The less people know the fewer ways they can hurt you. The fact is everyone doesn't need to know everything.

I'm so closed mouth about my drug selling endeavor that Dionna doesn't even know. I want to tell her just because we don't keep anything from one another, but I have an oath with AK that only people who need to know what we do will know. On the low, I want to tell her because I think she should know. On the other hand, she may judge me and not want to kick it with me. I'm just not willing to risk that. I'll tell her when I think the time is right.

"You ate?" I ask.

"No, I haven't, but I'm hungry though," she responds.

"True, me too. You tryin to eat up here or go off campus?" I inquire.

Dionna replies, "Umm, I don't know what they serving today."

I voice, "No doubt. Well, there's only one way to find out."

Dionna and I get up from the booth and walk over to the food line. We look at the selection of what's being served. There's baked chicken, pizza, and sandwiches just to name a few.

"What you thinking?" I ask.

"I'm thinking we should just grab something off campus," Dionna verbalizes.

"I'm down. Let's bounce," I utter.

Dionna and I collect our things from the booth and head to my whip. We make it to the whip and decide to grab something to eat off of Bloomfield Ave. There's a local restaurant named Nell's over there that sells the best steak and cheese sandwiches. We make it over to Nell's and enjoy a great lunch. It's filled with a lot of laughter and great conversation like always. While we're eating, my phone rings. I look at the screen and see that AK is calling. I'm not expecting a call from him, so I answer.

"Yo, what up nigga?" I ask.

"Normal shit. We need to get up. I'm trying to play ball today, but I need to go get a new Celtics jersey to play in," AK words.

"Bet, I didn't know you were trying to ball up today," I respond.

"Yeah, I wasn't at first, but a lot of these niggas was talking trash and I couldn't resist, so I told them I'd play ball with them. I'm not trying to be looking like a bum, so I want to get some fresh home jerseys. It might be some girls out there. I need you to ball up with me," AK narrates.

"If you balling, I'm definitely trying to ball up with you. Where you at?" I state enthusiastically.

"Cool, I'll be at the park in an hour," AK answers.

"True, I'm by campus getting some lunch, but we just finished eating, so I can head that way in a minute. I'll be out there in about an hour, hour and a half," I recite.

"Aight. I'll be at the park," AK informs.

We end the call. I tell Dionna that I'm going to St. Marks Park in Linden to meet up with AK to play basketball, but the truth is that I'm not going to play basketball. The real deal is that AK isn't the least bit concerned about playing basketball or buying a Celtic's jersey. A home Celtics jersey is white in color, so we use that to represent cocaine because we don't want to say cocaine over the phone. The away Celtics jersey is green, so we use that to represent marijuana when we speak over the phone. AK is letting me know that we have to pick up some cocaine from the connect.

Dionna and I drive back to campus. I walk her to her next class. We laugh and joke all the way there. On the low, I don't want to leave her side, but business is business. I can tell she doesn't want me to go either from the way she's hanging on my shoulder and every word.

"Aight, baby girl. It's time for me to slide out. About to hit the court and show these lil niggas what it is," I assert.

Dionna replies, "You better do your thing out there. Don't get your ankles broke. I don't wanna have to take care of you."

"Yeah whatever. You ain't never gonna see

me get my ankles broke. You wildin right now," I shoot back confidently.

"Boy whatever. Maybe that's why you never let me see you play. You don't want me to see you get crossed over," Dionna voices.

I state, "You buggin. I'm gonna let you see me play one day. In fact, you can ride to Linden with me now and see me ball up."

"Now, you the one bugging. You know I'm not missing my class for nothing. I don't play like that," Dionna remarks.

I respond as I hug her, "I know. I know. You be on your good girl stuff and that's why I'm feeling you the way I am."

Dionna speaks, as she wraps her hands around my waist, "Oh you feeling me? And how exactly are you feeling me?"

I joke, "I ain't feeling you. I mean, you aight, but you ain't all that."

Dionna pushes me away and states, "Whatever. You know I'm da bomb and that's why you feeling me."

"Yeah, yeah, whatever," I say.

Dionna asks, "Are you saying that I'm lying?"

I answer, "You know what it is."

Dionna utters, "That's what I thought. Well listen Babe, let me get to class. Hit me up later when you get finished."

I pull Dionna in close by her hips and say, "Aight Babe, have fun. I'm out."

I give Dionna a kiss and walk away. I head

back to the car feeling great. I feel like I'm on top of the world. My love life is batting a thousand, my health is fantastic, and my money is golden. I make it to the car and put on Murda Muzik. As I ride down the Parkway, I bump my system almost as loud as it will go. This CD always hypes me up. I'm a little surprised that AK hit me up so soon to meet up with the connect. We weren't supposed to be meeting with him again this soon, but it is what it is.

I pull up to the park and see AK shooting around with some of the kids in the park. I walk in the park to the court AK is on. He looks over at me and shoots another jump shot. The shot is bottom of the net. One of the kids in the park fetches the ball and throws it back to AK. He dribbles the ball and does some crossover and behind the back dribble.

"What up nigga?" AK asks.

"Ain't nothing. Just leaving campus. Came to see what you were talking about on the phone," I answer.

"True, we gotta go get them Jerseys later, but we'll holla in a second," AK says.

"No doubt," I voice as I walk toward the bleachers.

AK dribbles some more and shoots another jump shot. He boasts to the kids on the court. One kid gets another rebound and tosses AK the ball again. He's made a few shots in a row, so it's in his favor to start missing. I know AK can't turn down a bet, so I'm going to make a wager with him right now while winning the bet is in my favor.

"Brick!" I yell, as AK shoots.

AK misses the shot badly. He barely hit the rim on that shot. I knew his luck was bound to run out. I wish I could have bet him on that shot, but he was already in the motion. I know I got his ass now though. I know him well enough to know that he's going to want to make up for missing so poorly at the exact time I yelled out to him.

"Throw me the ball," AK says to the kid who got the rebound.

"For what? You know you just gonna shoot another brick!" I say antagonistically.

"Whateva, Rah. Put ya money up nigga," AK shoots back.

I reply arrogantly, "That ain't never been a problem. You call the number."

AK reaches in his pocket and throws a fifty-dollar bill to the ground. I walk over to the court and throw a fifty down on top of his. AK dribbles slowly to the top of the key. He lines himself up with the basket and dribbles a few more times. Seconds later, he shakes his head and goes to the corner of the court right behind the three-point line. He dribbles two times and takes the jump shot. The ball goes straight through the basket without touching the rim. It's nothing, but net. AK leaves his hand in the air and runs across the court and picks up his money. He laughs at me as he stuffs the money in his pocket.

"Nah, nigga. Run that shit back! You ain't getting to keep my dough in your pocket," I say quickly.

I take a hundred-dollar bill out of my pocket and throw it on the basketball court. AK's eyes get big when he sees that I've upped the bet. He takes the two fifty-dollar bills out his pocket and throws them on the ground. He begins dribbling the basketball again as he sizes up his next shot.

"You gonna let me take your money again?" AK asks cockily.

I remark, "Nah, you definitely about to shoot an air ball and you know those are double. Stop dribbling and shoot that shit nigga."

AK speaks, "I know it's double for an airball, but I'm not worried about that shit cause I ain't shooting no damn air ball. This shit bottom of the net."

"Pull up and stop talking then," I order.

AK goes to the same corner of the court that he made the first shot that enabled him to take my money. He takes his sweet time shooting the shot. AK begins doing fake measures of height and distance from himself to the basket.

"I just measured the wind velocity to calculate my shot. It looks like you bout to be out of a hundred dollars my nigga," AK boasts.

"Nigga, if you don't shoot the shot, I'm just

gonna pick my bread up and call it quits. You takin too damn long," I comment in a peeved tone.

AK replies, "Hell no! You ain't calling off the bet. The money already on the ground. It's gonna be in my pocket real soon though."

"Whatever son," I say.

AK finally shoots the jump shot. It rotates through the air perfectly and has the best arc I've ever seen. To my dislike, the shot goes in the basket flawlessly as did the first one. The net snaps as the ball falls to the ground. AK starts doing the running man on the court. He's really rubbing it in. AK does the running man all the way over to the money he has just won. Again, he stuffs the money in his pocket as he laughs at me.

"You wanna run it back again?" AK asks.

I answer, "Nah, I'm good. You need to holla at me anyway."

"Oh, just checking cause I could use another hunnet fifty off you. I can go buy some fresh butta softs with your money," AK boasts. "I definitely need to get at you."

"Word. I'm done with the betting for today. I'll get my bread back from your lucky ass like I always do," I voice.

AK takes another shot and misses. A kid chases the rebound and me and AK walk to the sitting area in the park to chat. We make it over to the sitting area and AK reaches in his pocket and pulls out a blunt. He also takes out a bag of weed. AK splits the blunt and empties its contents out on the ground.

"So, what's good with ole boy?" I inquire. "We weren't posed to get up with him this soon, right?"

"Dude said that he got the shit in early, so we gotta go pick it up today. He ain't tryna sit on that shit for too long," AK says as he puts the weed in the blunt.

"Oh word. I thought something was wrong. Dude don't normally call us early to pick the shit up," I say.

"No doubt. He said everything good. It ain't sound like anything was wrong. Normal shit," AK verbalizes.

"True, what he say about the bread we owe him for the last shipment? He's a week early, so I know he ain't trying to get his bread early too," I state.

AK lights his blunt and says, "He said we can give him what we got now and give him the rest later as scheduled."

I rub my chin and say, "Hmm, that seems outta pocket as hell. He switching shit up like a muh-fucker. He ain't never did no shit like this before."

AK comments, "You right. Sometimes shit happens differently. It seems like you thinking some funny shit is going down."

I vocalize, "I'm not saying that for sure, but

you know you're the only one I trust wholeheartedly. I'm just saying it's different and that should always make us a bit more cautious."

AK speaks, "I feel you. Well, if he's different on this one, then we move different on this one too."

"I'm feeling that. How you wanna move?" I ask.

"Dig, I'm thinking we can drive separate cars to Cherry Hill. You or me can go to his crib to pick the shit up. Bang, when whichever one of us gets the product and all is clear then we'll send the other the all clear. Then bring him his dough," AK explains as the smoke from his blunt blows through his nostrils.

"Right, right. So that way if he's on some funny shit, he won't have the money too. See that's why I fucks with you. Aight, that's what we gonna do," I articulate.

"You already know," AK says as he gives me a dap.

AK and I converse more as we sit on the bench. We decide to go to see the connect in south Jersey at six o'clock because we want it to still be light outside. I'll drive down to pick up the new product and AK will leave thirty minutes behind me carrying the money. We don't want to be on the road side by side and a cop notices us and becomes suspicious. The plan is I'll pick up the product and leave Gary's house and call AK to tell him he can drop the money off. AK finishes smoking his blunt and then we depart the park to get things in order for the drive.

# CHAPTER 7

I'm riding south on the turnpike headed to Cherry Hill. AK is sticking to the plan and is leaving Linden thirty minutes behind me. I'm not driving my everyday whip to get to the connect's house. I have a Sentra that I drive that's non-descript and won't draw any attention. The traffic isn't heavy and I'm making great time. I'll be at ole boy's house in no time. My phone starts ringing while I'm driving. I look at the phone and see it's my baby girl calling. I answer the phone.

I ask, "What's up Babe? How you?"

"I'm good. Just chilling in the dorm. What you doing?" Dionna inquires.

I answer, "I'm just cooling. I'm following AK to drop his car off. He wants to get his windows tinted."

"True, but I thought he already has his

windows tinted," Dionna says.

I pause for a second because she's right. AK definitely has tinted windows. I lied to her because I obviously can't tell her where I'm going or what I'll be doing. I have to tell her something that's not going to alarm her of something being awry. She's not the least bit slow, so I know she's not going to just accept any answer. I'm not a dull pencil either, so I know I'll tell her something that will satisfy her question.

"Duh, I know he already has tints, but he said they aren't dark enough. He said too many people be looking in his whip and he's not feeling that," I orate.

"Oh my goodness! You know ya boy is always so extra. All he does is find ways to waste money," Dionna mentions.

I respond, "Yeah, I know, but it's his money and he lives how he wants to live. I think the tints will just get him pulled over more than he already does."

"I know that's right. You only speaking the truth," Dionna voices.

"Yeah, you know how it goes. But I'm gonna call you later. I don't wanna get caught talking on the phone. You know the fine is heavy," I word.

"Okay Babe, I love you," Dionna says.

I state, before I end the call, "I love you too baby."

I really don't care about a punk ass ticket for driving while being on the phone. I just want to focus on meeting with the connect. I always overthink things and I'm hoping that this is just one of those cases. We'll find out what it is in a hot minute. I wonder if AK is on the road already. I call AK to check on his whereabouts.

"Yo, what's the word?" I ask.

"Shit, it's all good. I'm on the turnpike. I'll be down there in a minute," AK answers.

"Bet, that's what it is. I'll be at ole boy's house in a few minutes," I tell.

"Aight, you want me to just pull up or wait at the gas station that you met your girl at?" AK asks.

"Umm, nah. Dig it. You remember the spot where we met those twins from Philly at?" I ask.

"Of course I do. Them bitches were bad as hell! I won't ever forget that shit my nigga," AK comments enthusiastically.

"Hell yeah, them broads were freaks! I want you to go there and I'll hit you up to let you know what it is," I verbalize.

"Say no more my nigga. I'll be there," AK assures.

I hang up the phone as I'm pulling up to the connect's house. As I'm about to call him, the garage door begins to rise. I guess he's really looking forward to seeing me today. This guy must've been looking out his window for me. I find it suspicious, but I still pull into the garage. This game is tricky and you never know who or what is moving against you. I put the car in park and get out.

"Gary, what's good fam?" I ask as I walk towards him.

"Normal shit Rah. Just trying to get y'all straight," he answers.

"I feel you on that. I didn't expect to see you so soon. I was surprised as hell when my man said you wanted to meet early. He would've come with me, but he got caught up with a broad. Either way, I'm here," I narrate.

Gary replies, "You know your boy is wild as hell. He always got bitches on deck. And my bad on calling early. The shit came in early, so I figured I'd let y'all know. Plus, I'm gonna be outta town on vacay soon."

"Yeah, my boy stays with the bitches. Good looks on letting us know," I say as I look around.

Gary voices, "Shit, nigga you got bitches too! Don't front. I already know."

"Nah, I got one girl and that's it, but what's good with what you got for me?" I inquire abruptly.

"It's in the trunk of my whip in the duffle bags like normal. Damn bra, you good?" Gary asks.

"I'm straight. Just tryna get through. Got a lot of shit on my mind and on the ride down I got hot as hell," I answer.

You gonna be good for the ride back? You want me to grab you a water or soda from the fridge," Gary inquires.

"Nah, I'm good. Just gonna ride with the

windows down," I vocalize.

I didn't mean to be short with Gary, but I'm not here for the small talk. This is the part of the game that I don't like. It's so much uncertainty. For all I know, this dude could be setting me up. I can't help but to think that as soon as I take possession of this shit that something is going to pop off. At the same time, I could just be tripping. The nigga did say he's going out of town. I walk over to the trunk and look through the bags. Everything's like normal, so I throw the bags in my trunk.

"Aight, I can't force you to stay hydrated. I can go get you something. It's nothing," Gary replies.

"I'm good on the beverage for real. Yo, the load looks proper, but listen, we gonna have to bring you the bread later," I say.

"What you mean? Your boy said you'd give me whatever bread you had for me today when we met up," Gary shoots back.

"Yeah, and we'll get it to you tonight. You called us last minute and we came through to take the product off your hands and I'm doing that now. But as far as the bread is concerned, you know it takes some time to put it together. AK stayed up the way and is waiting with his chick for some more money to come through," I explain.

"Damn, I wish you would've told me. I was expecting something now. I told AK that I would take what y'all had," Gary chimes in.

"True, I feel you, but it'll only be a little while longer. You know what, I'll leave the shit here and we'll pick it up when we bring you your dough some other time," I state.

"Oh nah, you can take the shit. I know I put y'all in a fucked-up spot when I called. I just got to eat that. It's on me, so I'll just wait til later to get the dough. Keeping it real, you doing me a favor by taking it off my hands," Gary offers.

"Aight, that's what it is. Dig, we'll hit you in a while to let you know we're bringing the money," I say.

"Aight, fam. Hit me up," Gary speaks.
"Shit, let me call AK real quick and see what it's hittin for," I comment.

Gary voices, "That's a good look. Hit him up. I could use that bread ASAP for my vacation. I can leave earlier than expected."

"Yo, I'm bout to finish up. Oh shit! That's what's up! You already down here. Bet, come through to Gary spot. Oh word, I feel you. I'll meet you there. Aight one," I say to AK on the phone.

"Sounds like good news to me," Gary says excitedly.

"Yeah, it is AK got some ends for you. When I told him to come through, he said he didn't want another car to pull up to ya spot and make it hot, so Imma meet him and we gonna ride back over," I explain.

"Bet, that's what it is! I'll be here. Get at me," Gary utters.

"Yo, let me fuck with that soda you offered. Let a nigga get some ice too. My mouth is dry as hell," I voice as I chuckle.

Gary laughs and goes inside the house. Moments later he returns with a red cup with ice in it and a bottle of Pepsi. I dap Gary up and jump in the car. The garage door opens and I back out of the driveway. I hope this ain't no damn setup for real. AK has to be wondering what's going on by now. Let me hit him up. I start driving to where I told AK to go.

"Yo, what's good?" I ask.

"Shit, you know what it is. I'm waiting on you. Was thinking I should hit you up. Was seeming like it was taking a long time," AK says.

"Everything smooth. Ain't shit happen, but I'm headed to you now. I'll holla at you when I get over there. Are you real close to the meet up spot yet?" I ask.

"Oh word. Yeah, I'm like right in the same spot," AK answers.

"Hell yeah. Give me a few minutes. Yo, do me a favor. Put the money on the ground by the support post you're parked closest to and keep an eye on it. I'm gonna pull up and drop the bag that I got from Gary and pull off. You get my bag and bounce and I'll get yours and take it to Gary," I detail.

A few minutes later, I make it over to where

AK is parked at. I told him to wait for me in the Cherry Hill Mall parking garage just to be on the safe side. If it was a setup, I didn't want us to get jammed up. This way, I'm really the only one that will have to explain myself. I pull into a space near AK and drop the bag. I see him looking at me and he looks toward the post where he dropped the money bag. I drive over there and jump out the car to retrieve it.

I drive out of the parking lot and start heading back to Gary's place. I call Gary to let him know that his money is on its way. He's souped up that I'm bringing him his bread. I call AK from my other phone to make sure he's good.

"You got the bag?" I ask.

"Oh yeah, we good. I'm gonna head back to Linden if you're good," he says.

"I'm good. I'll drop him his bread and be on the turnpike ASAP. I'll meet you in Linden later," I reply.

"Bet, yo you got a crazy mind. Holla at me," AK says as he chuckles.

I hang up and drive back to Gary's crib. As I'm driving, I look in my rear-view mirror and don't see anything suspicious. Everything is flowing smoothly. I definitely overthought this one. However, it's better to be safe than to be sorry. I pull into the parking lot of the gas station that Dionna works at and out of nowhere several police officers surround my car. They're in marked and unmarked cars and have their guns drawn on me.

I keep my hands on the steering wheel and don't move. They rush to the driver's side of my vehicle and tell me to step out of the car. I keep my hands raised in the air, but I don't move. The cops open the car door and pull me out of the car. They throw me on the hood of the car and search me. I'm not the least bit worried because I don't have anything on me that I shouldn't. The cops ask me for permission to search the car and I grant it. The police immediately search the trunk of my car. They open the black duffle bag that I picked up from AK that has the cash in it that we were supposed to give Gary. They ask me where I got the money from and I tell them that I got the money from the bank.

All of the cops laugh hysterically at my answer. They think because I'm young that I can't have thirty thousand dollars. I notice that the cops are still looking for something. It dawns on me that they're looking for the drugs that I do not have. They eventually look in the backseat to see if they can find what they want. If only they knew that those drugs are tucked and not in my possession, they would save themselves some headache.

"Officers, what have I done wrong? Why have I been pulled over?" I inquire as I sit on the curb.

"Well, one of our state troopers saw you drive past a short while ago and then you came back again. Additionally, we had a report of some suspicious activity in the area and quite frankly you seem suspicious to us," Officer Brantley says.

"Sorry I've caused you guys to waste your time, but nothing suspicious is going on with me" I tell.

"Well, that's the reason we're with you currently and we're just following up on a report. And for you to have thirty thousand dollars cash in your trunk tells us something is going on," Officer Brantley voices.

"My girlfriend lives down here, so that's why I'm down here and as far as the money is concerned, I'm going to switch banks, so I withdrew money from my account," I explain.

"Fellas, this guy says he withdrew the money from his account. He really wants us to believe that he had thirty-grand in the bank," Officer Brantley tells as he chuckles.

The other cops that he's with all start laughing at me. They are pointing at me like I'm a joke. The interesting thing is that I'm actually telling the truth about the money coming out of my account. AK and I have a joint account that enables us to justify some of the money we have. If we're ever challenged about money we have, the account is our safeguard. We spend the money we make selling drugs on bills and other things we want.

"No, I'm for real Officer. The bank withdrawal information is sitting on the passenger's seat of my car. It's no joke," I yell out.

Officer Brantley tells one of the other officers to check the front seat of my car for the bank receipt. He doesn't say anything to me, while one of the other officers searches. A moment later, the cop emerges from my car holding a white slip. He brings it over to Officer Brantley. Officer Brantley looks over the bank slip and is surprised.

"I see you're not lying about the bank withdrawal. Just a word of advice going forward, next time get a cashier's check. It's much safer than carrying a boatload of money," he says.

I voice, "I guess carrying the money is risky, but I'm not too familiar with the banking system. I am just more familiar with money, so I took it out. I would've gone straight to the bank, but I wanted to show off my money to my girlfriend."

"I've been there many times before. I've made many mistakes trying to impress women in my day. I'm gonna stand you up and get those cuffs off of you," Officer Brantley says.

I stand up as the officer helps me to my feet. Before he uncuffs me, he asks the cops one more time if they've found anything illegal. The cops shake their heads indicating that the car is clean. Next, he uncuffs me. The handcuffs slightly cut my wrists, so I begin massaging them while I walk back to the car. I walk to the trunk of my car to make sure my bag was still there and filled my cash. I check the bag and it all seems to be there. I close the trunk and walk to my car door.

As I'm walking, the officer calls out, "By the

way, what's your girlfriend's name? You stated that she lives in Cherry Hill, right?"

"I don't see why you need her name, but it's Dionna Chambers," I yell out.

"Just checking one last piece of your story is all. Hold up one more second for me," Officer Brantley says.

He asks me how to spell her name and then goes in his patrol unit. I see he's typing in his computer. A few minutes later, he gets out of his car and tells me that my information checks out and that I'm free to leave. I get in my car and drive away. I wave at the police officers in a friendly gesture as I pass by them. I glance at my phone and see that AK has called me several times. I know he's wondering what happened to me. I call him back immediately.

"Yo," I say as he answers the call.

AK voices, "Nigga I'm glad you good! I started to turn around to see if you were good, but I didn't cause I got…"

"Nigga, I just got pulled the fuck over! The fucking pigs came from out of nowhere. It had to be at least ten cars. I was like what the fuck is goin on," I orate as I cut AK's speech off.

AK shouts wildly, "Yo, that's crazy as hell! I knew some other shit happened when you missed all those calls. Nigga you not gonna believe this shit though!"

"Nigga, don't say you got pulled too!" I vocalize excitedly.

AK shoots back, "Hell to the fucking yeah! They ran down on me like six cars deep and yanked my black ass out the car and searched it. Da crazy shit is that they found the duffle bag, but it only had some clothes in it. No product. I was confused and happy as fuck."

"Yo, fuck the police. Them bastards ain't smart as us. Meet me at the Marks, so we can poly this shit," I state.

"Aight, I'm headed there now, but you good?" AK inquires.

"Oh yeah, I'm gravy. They held me and searched the car. They found the bread, but they ain't keep it I told them about the bank receipt and it all checked out. The one pig gave me some advice and let me go," I tell.

"That's what the fuck it is!" AK boasts.

"Hell yeah. When you came up with the idea to pull the money out the account that was dope as hell. That's the only reason he let me go. If not for that, I think they would've arrested me and took the money. Nigga, you a genius," I articulate.

"Shit, I don't know about that genius shit, but we both nice as hell at what we do. But dig, I'll meet you at the park," AK says.

"Holla at ya boy. I'll be out there," I reply.

# CHAPTER 8

I pull up to the park and go sit on the bleachers. I'm just sitting here reflecting on how bad everything could've turned out. They really could've put me in cuffs and carted me away to jail. That would've been a tragedy. I'm glad it went my way because prison isn't where I want to be. AK pulls up to the park and walks over to me.

"My nigga," I say as I dap him up. "You saved me from going to jail today."

"Nigga, that shit ain't bout nuthin. That's how we roll. You got me and I got you. All day, every day," AK replies. "Nigga, you gotta tell me what happened at Gary's."

"Yo, I was uneasy when I was at that bitch ass nigga's spot. I pictured the cops running down on me with the shit in the trunk," I explain.

AK says, "Aight, I know that. Tell me some

shit I don't know."

"Nigga, I got you.  So, I fake called you and told Gary that me and you were gonna double right back with his cash.  He was all in, so I left and came to where you were," I tell.

AK offers, "So boom, but you had no way of knowing if they'd grab you when you were on ya way to me."

"Right, I didn't, so after I loaded the shit in my trunk, I sent Gary in the kitchen to get me some fluids," I convey.

AK cuts me off and blurts out, "And you took the shit out the trunk and stashed it in his fucking garage!"

Before I have a chance to respond to AK, he takes off running down the bleachers in excitement.  He is laughing and screaming as he covers his mouth.  Seconds later, AK runs back up the bleachers and daps me up several times. He even gives me a hug.  This is AK's normal. He's always exaggerated and animated.

"Hell yeah, that shit is still in that bitch ass nigga's own garage.  He don't even know it.  Him and the cops are still sitting somewhere confused as hell," I word proudly.

"Shit, nigga! I was confused as hell too.  I knew I was going to jail for sure.  You said that I kept you from going to jail.  Nah, nigga you saved me!" AK yells out happily.

"Nigga, you know we gotta protect each other out here.  It's how we keep gettin this fuckin guap," I speak.

"Oh no doubt!  And we have nothing to lose by leaving it at Gary's.  If we did get pulled over, we wouldn't have the drugs on us and if nothing happened, we could always retrieve the coke from Gary's spot," AK details.

I respond, "Exactly!  That was my thinking.  My bad, I didn't tell you on the phone.  Shit was moving so fast that I just told myself I'd tell you later."

"Man, I don't give a fuck about that shit!  You made a move at the spur of the moment to benefit us.  Nigga, we golden!" AK replies.

"No doubt.  That's what's up!  Son, we gotta figure this shit out for real though.  That getting pulled over shit got me fucked up," I say.

"Yo, the nigga Gary called me after I hung up with you and told me he saw you pulled over.  I didn't talk to him for long cause I didn't know what type shit he was on," AK verbalizes.

"Son, he had to set that shit up.  Ain't no way they swarmed on us like that for nothing.  That's why he probably called for us to pick the shit up early.  He wanted to set us the fuck up!" I dictate angrily.

"Yo, I was on the same damn thoughts.  That shit is too coincidental," AK shoots back.  "He had to put that shit into play."

"I know, but then I was thinking it don't make sense for him to give us the shit to only call the cops on us.  He loses all way around.  Plus, the cops could've pulled me over when I was leaving his house if that were the case," I explain while perplexed.

"I feel you, but peep this. Maybe he had already been caught getting the drugs from whomever he buys from. Then the cops told him to set up whoever moves the drugs for him. That would be us. You probably threw their plan off when you didn't have the money and then said you were meeting me, so they waited and were gonna scoop us up once the money got dropped," AK speculates.

"Yeah, that's gotta be it, but it's a lot of ways it could've went. I know I'm not fucking with him like that though. It's over," I say.

"Oh, no doubt. He said on the phone that he wants his money that we owe him and the money for the new shit. I told him I don't know what he's talking about just in case he had the police on the line," AK informs. "He was mad as hell when I said that."

"That nigga gotta know that he ain't getting shit from us. That shit is over. I ain't even trying to talk to him again. For all I know, he set that shit up. That snake ass nigga is just beat. He gotta hold that L," I voice.

"Good, then we on the same page. I already copped another burner, but I haven't dumped the old burner yet. I hope you dumped yours though," AK says.

"Nah, not yet. I'm getting one today though,

so I can put all the contacts in it. Then, I'll dump it," I tell.

"That's what it is! Same with me. Just know that we gonna have to be on point after this. That nigga might try to retaliate," AK says.

I respond, "I know, but that's part of the game. We signed up for this shit a long time ago."

In his Tony Montana voice AK says, "If you want to go to war, I'll take you to war."

"Right, right. You know we bout to come off crazy! We got all the shit from the last shipment and we gonna eat off that. Gary ain't getting none of that bread," I state excitedly.

"Yeah, my nigga. I know. We gonna be able to make some crazy moves after this. It's our time!" AK calls out.

"Word. I'm bout to head to campus to see Dionna. I'll holla at you next day my nigga. Keep your head on a swivel," I say.

I walk away from AK and get in his car. We're switching cars because he's going to secure the money at our stash spot. I drive through Roselle to get on the parkway. I'm not taking the local route to campus right because sometimes the scenic route takes too long and I'm exhausted. My phone starts ringing as I'm getting on the parkway.

"What's good Babe?" I ask.

"You and me," Dionna counters.

"You know I like the sound of that. I was just

about to call you. I was gonna wait til I got on the Parkway," I tell.

"Da Parkway? Where you going? You about to tell me that you're coming to see me?" Dionna asks.

"Yes, baby. I'm coming to see you. I wasn't going another minute without seeing you. Nope, no way in hell," I comment.

"Oh okay. I was about to say," Dionna responds.

"You wasn't bout to say nothing. In fact, we're fighting when I get there," I say jokingly.

"Yeah, yeah. Whatever. You know I don't play boy," Dionna replies. "Hurry your big head self up too. I miss you," she says warmly.

"I miss you too. I'll hit you when I get outside your dorm," I communicate.

"Okay, later," she speaks.

"Later," I word.

I hang up with Dionna and continue driving. It's a cool Jersey night, so I'm riding with the windows down and sunroof open. I've always enjoyed driving by myself because it gives me time to reflect, strategize, and put things into perspective. I probably need a longer drive than normal for all I have on my mind. I'm at a crazy crossroad in my life. I'm heavily considering giving the drug trafficking game up and just falling back from it. I've got enough paper saved up that I can just chill. Besides that, I'm still working and going to school. I only have three more semesters of school left and then I'll have my degree in hand. I'll definitely be able to find gainful employment. There have been too many close calls with me and the police. I know it's only a matter of time before my luck runs out. It's time to have a serious talk with myself. I'm sure there are some dudes who had success in the drug game and never got caught, but they are few and far in between. The longer I stay in the game, the better my chances of getting locked in a cage become. What am I to do? I pull up to campus and walk over to Russ Hall which is the dorm Dionna stays in. I call her from the front of the dorm and she comes to get me.

"Hey, Babe," Dionna voices, as she walks over to me.

"Honey, damn you have an extra glow to you tonight. Look like you got water glistening all over your body," I say jokingly. "Let's walk and talk. It's mad nice out here. I don't want to chill in the room."

"It's all your fault that I'm glowing like this. You got my nose all open from treating me so good. Okay, I'm down. I been in the room for forever working on a paper. I need some air," Dionna says.

"That's what it is, but you were glowing when I first saw you. Shit, that's what attracted me to you. Keeping it real," I remark.

"Yeah, you probably right, but I was glowing because I'm fine as hell, educated, and my outlook on life in general is positive," Dionna explains.

I cut her off and voice, "Oh so you just all that from what it sounds. Damn, I know you're fly as hell, but damn. You sound like you shine like the sun."

"Boy, you so stupid," Dionna says as she laughs and slaps me playfully. "No seriously, you make me glow differently…almost like an inner glow. It's a glow that men just can't understand and it's not easily put into words. It's a feeling of loving someone and knowing that that person loves you back. It's a very refreshing and reassuring thing. I don't know if that makes sense, but that's what it is."

"So, who exactly is it that loves you?" I ask while chuckling.

Dionna pops me in the back of the head for my comment. I take off running and she takes off after me. I stop running and curl up into a ball. Dionna is pinching and poking me all over my body. I'm flinching left and right as she pokes me in all my vulnerable areas. I can't stop laughing. Dionna grabs me by my ear and I'm completely at her mercy.

"Chill D. Chill. I was just playing!" I yell out.

"You bet your ass that you were just playing. Go ahead and say it before I pull your ear off," Dionna orders sternly.

"What? I'm sorry," I shoot back in a hurry.

Dionna pulls my ear tighter, as she asks, "Who

loves me?"

"I do! I love you! Come on, I said it. You can let my ear go," I bellow as I laugh loudly.

"That's what I thought boy. You were trying to play me out. You know you love me to death, so stop playing," Dionna utters.

I pull Dionna close to me and hug her. She looks me in my eyes and I look back at her. I clear her hair from off her eyelash and give her a kiss under the moonlight. After we kiss, she rests her head on my shoulder and I hold her.

"Nah, but on the real though. You know I love you. That's real. I love the time we spend together and I don't want to be anywhere other than with you," I verbalize.

"I know you do. And I love you too. The feeling is definitely mutual. See, you can't be talking to me like this. This is why I'm glowing inside and it shines outward," Dionna responds.

We continue walking the campus of Montclair State University as we chop it up. Dionna tells me about the paper she had to write and I tell her about some discussions I had in class. I wish I could put her on to the craziness that went on with me and the police, but I wouldn't even know where to start. One good thing is that I'm not as worked up about things as I was before I linked up with her. She always calms my nerves without knowing it. Just being with her is like an elixir for soothing pain and worry. There's no wonder why I hold her in such high regard.

"I guess we shine together. I'm good with that," I communicate.

I'm parked right outside Dionna's dorm and I'm about to bounce, so she walks me to my car. I'm leaned up against the driver's side door of the car and Dionna's body is tightly pressed up against mine. We start out giving each other small peck kisses on the lips and that evolves into sensual tongue kissing with a lot of groping. Dionna and I eventually end up getting in the car and having an all-out sex session. The car is rocking back and forth as we're pleasuring each other. The air is filled with grunts, moans, and slaps as we get right. My car windows are fogged up and we can't see out of them. We are both dripping with sweat as we finish our session. We're catching our breath in the backseat of my car.

"You are so bad! I can't believe you got me out here like this. I've never even came close to having sex in the car before. I mean it was good, but it just ain't my style. I can't front though, I now see why people do it," Dionna narrates as she continues to breathe heavily.

I reply, "Don't try to put this on me. As far as I'm concerned, you pulled me into the car. It was all your work."

I clear one of my windows because I want to look outside. I see several people walking around. I don't know why all these people are walking around this late. I've never seen this many people walking around at this time. I look around some more and see a police officer walking towards my car.

"Oh shit! D, get dressed. A pig is walking this way," I yell.

"Boy, please tell me you playing!" Dionna shoots back in a panic.

We both grab our clothes and throw them on in a hurry. As I'm sliding my pants on, I look out the window and see what the cop is doing. He's stopped by a car looking at the windshield. I guess he's checking parking permits. Dionna and I get our clothes back on and we climb in the front seat. Seconds later, the cop shines his flashlight inside my car. He motions for me to roll my window down.

"Hi officer," I say.

"Hi, is everything alright in here?" He asks, as he looks at Dionna.

"Yes sir. Everything is fine. Just hanging with my boyfriend before he leaves campus," Dionna words.

"Okay, enjoy the night and be safe," the officer says.

"Thank you. You do the same," I state.

I roll the window up and the cop walks away. I look over at Dionna and she lets out a sigh of relief. Ten years of stress just disappeared from her face. She smacks me on my arm.

"Boy, I was shook outta my mind. I saw my scholarship getting flushed down the toilet. I'm telling you I almost started to cry," Dionna tells.

"Nah, you would've been good regardless," I reply.

"Umm, I don't know about that. My mom would've cursed me out and cried. My brother Derek would've killed me. He would have left his duty station in Hawaii just to check me. You know they're crazy protective to begin with and if they would've heard that I lost my scholarship over having car sex, they would've strangled me together," Dionna conveys passionately.

"I feel you, but I would've worked out something with your tuition. It's only money, so you would've been fine. I got a few dollars tucked for an emergency. Sounds like you have a caring family that holds you accountable," I respond.

"Boy, I know you work, but this tuition is something serious. And yes, my fam is da bomb! You'll meet them when the time is right. My mom and brother don't like to meet guys I date right away because they say niggas are a dime a dozen. My mom knows the games that dudes run, so she waits to see how long they stick around before she meets them," Dionna communicates.

I respond, "I got your back on that tuition, so you would've been fine. I feel your peeps on that because I don't like to meet a lot of people myself. Just like to keep to the people I know."

"Yeah, I know. You don't like to meet

nobody. You mad anti-social, but it's cool though. I like having you basically to myself," Dionna offers.

That's real. Look at you not wanting to share me. I always knew you were selfish," I comment sarcastically.

"Damn right I'm selfish, but only when it comes to sharing my man with the rest of the world," Dionna says.

I voice, "I ain't mad at ya. Well, I'm bout to hit the crib. I got like a two-page paper to type up for class tomorrow and I gotta work in the morning."

"Okay, big head! Hit me up in the morning," Dionna states.

"You like my big head, don't you?" I ask.

"You are such a freak! Wasn't nobody even talking about your dick, even though it is kinda big," Dionna speaks.

"You right. I am a freak, but only for you and my dick is big. I'll hit you in the morning for sure. Soon as I wake up," I convey.

"You want me to walk you to your dorm?" I ask.

"Naw, I'm good. It's right there, but you can watch me until I walk inside if it's really on your heart," Dionna answers.

Dionna leans over and gives me a hug and a kiss on the cheek. She gets out the car and starts walking to her dorm. As she walks, she struts as if she's on a model runway. Her booty is juggling with every step she takes. I guess she wants to give me a show as she walks away. I'm glad she's performing for me because I love the sight of her sexy ass. I tap the horn to the rhythm of the strides she's taking to let her know that I'm looking and I'm impressed. Dionna looks back at me and is cracking up. She's laughing harder than I am. When she looks back at me, I rapidly clap my hands to show my approval. Dionna doesn't let up. She does her exaggerated stroll until she reaches her dormitory vestibule. I drive away and head home. I needed her company after the drama I've had.

# CHAPTER 9

I'm sitting in the park in the play area for little kids. My niece is two years old and I'm babysitting for the day. She's having a ball running around and exploring. I wish there were some other kids out here for her to play with, but she's having fun, so I guess that's all that counts. AK is sitting in his car smoking a blunt. He's being considerate by not smoking around her. My niece falls in the dirt pretty hard. I jump up off the bench and run over to her. She doesn't cry from the impact instead she just looks at me. I think she's waiting to see how I respond to her falling to determine if she's going to cry. I pick her up and dust her off without making a big deal out of it. I put her back on the ground and she takes off running. I hear AK's car door close.

"It's about time you finished. You had to have rolled and smoked two of them. You was in

122

there for like three days," I joke.

AK says as he jumps the fence, "Nah, it was only one, but I had to curse a nigga out."

"Yeah? Who? It was one of your jump's boyfriends again?" I ask sarcastically.

"Man, I wish it was," AK answers as he daps me up.

"True, so what's the deal then? What's good?" I ask.

"Yo, that nigga Gary been calling me like a lil bitch. I'm starting to get tired of his shit. Fam, it's too much," AK replies.

"Gary? Fuck you mean Gary? He ain't get the picture yet?" I inquire in a puzzled tone.

"Right! That's what the fuck I'm saying. I have no idea why he keeps calling. I answered once cause it wasn't from his number," AK voices angrily.

"Son, that's crazy as hell! I hope he don't really think we still fuckin wit him. If he does, he's off his rocker. I'm coppin a new celly today," I state.

"Crazy shit yo! I got two new burners in my whip. I got one for you. I just gotta get the numbers outta it. This nigga talking some he want his money from us or he gonna have to take action on the street level. He was talking some put us in body bags type shit," AK conveys.

"Good looks on the burner. Say word my nigga! Wow! Old boy threatened to kill us. He's bugging. Nigga lost his fucking mind," I shoot back.

"Yo, I started yelling at the nigga and cursing him out, but that shit was pointless. I ended up hanging up on him," AK tells.

My side phone starts ringing from a number that's not programmed in my phone. I wonder who fuck it is. I normally don't answer numbers I don't know, but with the Gary situation present, I go ahead and answer it.

"Hello. Who dis?" I ask.

"Yo, this Gary man. I'm trying to get this situation back to good terms before it gets ugly. I just need my money and it's over after that," Gary articulates calmly.

I say, "Yo, I don't know anybody named Gary and I don't owe anybody any money. I got pulled over by the cops the other day and they took the only money I had."

"Son, don't play fucking stupid with me. I'm getting my bread one way or the other. I ain't recording this call and ain't nobody listening, so cut the bullshit fam! I know you both got pulled over and I also know they didn't confiscate your money or the product you bitch ass nigga," Gary explains violently.

"I got your bitch ass nigga. Ain't gonna be too much more of that slick shit you talking either. You must be the police if you know they didn't take my money or whatever product you talking bout. Have a nice day officer and don't call my number anymore," I shoot back.

"Nigga, if you hang up the phone, I'm telling you it's gonna get ugly for you. I promise you that. And I ain't no fucking police," Gary charges.

I reply, "Son, it's over. I don't have your money or ya product and I never did, but you can contact your local…"

AK snatches the phone out of my hand before I can finish my statement. The phone falls to the ground. AK quickly picks it up and puts it to his face.

"Nigga, you still there? Yo, I told you before. Fuck whatever money you think we owe you and fuck you too. You da police and if you not, fuck you cause it damn sure seem like you a pig! Fuck all this talking!" AK screams into the phone.

"Y'all niggas is bitch niggas. You ain't built for this life. Y'all niggas ain't real street niggas. Y'all niggas is good niggas who sell drugs, but that's what it is. I'll be seeing you and your bitch ass boy sooner than later. You better believe that!" Gary yells.

"Man whatever. You ain't talking bout nothing. Fuck around and get ya ass left stinking," AK voices as he ends the call.

I say, "Yo, that nigga is retarded as hell! He said he knows the police didn't take the money or the product from us. He seemed very certain of that. Son, he had to put the police up to pulling us over."

"Hell yeah, he did. That was too much of a

coincidence. He changed the money drop and pickup day and magically all that shit happened. He probably owes the cops some money or something and that was his way of paying them back. Ain't no telling fam, but it was definitely some funny shit!" AK vocalizes.

"True, I'm feeling you on that. I'm trying to figure if Gary is really dumb enough to try to move on us," I say as I rub my chin.

"Look at it like this. We didn't give him the money that he wanted early and we would've owed him more bread on that. Then turn around and he gave us more work that we ain't giving him no bread for. So basically, we got a whole lotta free money. I don't know how'd he'd move, but if I were him, I'd want to kill us. Not only that, I'd give it my best effort to do so," AK communicates.

"True. You right, so we gotta expect the worst or we could just pay the nigga and tell him his shit is in the garage. Ain't like we don't got the dough. It may not be worth the potential drama," I speak frankly.

"Man, but if we turn over the bread and he is the police then we're guilty of drug trafficking. They'd basically have us caught red-handed," AK explains.

"Damn! It's either one or the other. Risk going to jail or risk our lives. I ain't trying to be dead or in jail," I speak.

"Me either. We ain't gonna be either one of

them. We just gotta stay on point and we'll be good. Don't get caught slipping my nigga," AK says.

I voice, "Oh hell no. I ain't never getting caught slipping. That shit ain't happening. Just thinking forward…we gonna have to get a new connect from somewhere."

"No doubt. We'll definitely get a new supplier. But yo, keep the gat on you at all times cause I'm gonna have mine with me. Better Gary than either one of us. I know you feel me on that," AK voices.

"I'm definitely keepin da toast on me. Damn, I don't want to, but I will. I hate riding around with the gat. It is what it is though. Dig, I'm about to go change my niece and wash her up. Plus, I gotta go get the gat and me and Dionna taking my niece to Chucky Cheese on 22," I utter.

AK speaks, "Aight my nigga. You be safe out here in these streets.

"Yo, before I go, I gotta know if you trust me," I state.

"That's a dumb fucking question nigga! Of course I do! Hell yeah I do. With my life!" AK verbalizes sternly.

I comment, "That's good shit my nigga! I trust you with mine too. Yo, with that being said, I'm thinking we should play this one safe."

"Word? Play it safe how? What you got in mind?" AK inquires.

"I'm thinking we call or I can call this nigga

back and tell him where da shit is in his garage and work out a way to get him his bread. We'll be done with him and find another supplier," I explain.

"Keeping it all the way funky, I don't like it, but if you think that's the best move, I'm wit it," AK says.

"Word up I do. We won't have to watch our backs," I voice.

"Shit, my nigga! Make the call. You just saved me from going to jail, so I trust ya judgment. I ain't talking to the nigga though," AK declares.

I respond, "Aight! Shit, nigga I ain't making the call either. Imma get a random to make the call. That's what it do! I'll let you know what da deal is."

I peace AK up and grab my niece Jen and put her in her car seat. While we're driving to my crib, I call Gary to settle this situation. Unfortunately, he doesn't answer my call. Next, I call Dionna and tell her to meet me at the crib. Five minutes into the drive I look back and notice my niece is fast asleep. I guess the playground really wore her out. I pull up to my block and notice that Dionna's car is in front. I'm happy that she's here. I park the car and pull my niece out of her car seat. Dionna approaches us.

"Hey, big head," Dionna says as she kisses me on the cheek.

"What's good ma? How you?" I ask.

"Nothing, just getting outta class for the most

part. I ran a couple of errands, but nothing major," Dionna answers.

"True, I ain't been doing much either. I went to work this morning, but didn't make it to class because my brother needed me to keep Jen, so that's why I asked you about Chucky Cheese," I explain.

"Gotcha, well it looks like that move is on hold because she is passed out. I hope she wakes up soon," Dionna says.

I speak, "Yeah, she was running wild in the park. As soon as her bottom touched the car seat, she was out like a light."

"That's so funny. And she is so precious. I hope know you are a natural carrying her. You haven't even disrupted her sleep one bit," Dionna mentions.

I state, "Here you go. I ain't no natural. You on your baby tip again. It's too soon for all of that."

"Oh my goodness. You are so baby paranoid. If anybody mentions you and a baby you be all shook," Dionna jokes. "Trust me, I don't want any babies yet. I have to finish school and save some money."

"I ain't paranoid. I just ain't trying to front like I want kids now. You gonna have my seeds one day. Watch!" I orate.

"Well, we can practice on that when you put your niece down. I need some of you right now. I want it hard and I want it swift," Dionna verbalizes.

We make it into the apartment and Dionna cleans Jen up for me. Jen is still sleeping soundly while getting cleaned up. I go to the bathroom and wash myself up in preparation for giving Dionna the business. A few minutes later, Dionna comes into the bathroom. She strips down and I attempt to please her sexually. She pushes me away from her and turns on the shower. Dionna jumps in the shower and I go to check on Jen as she sleeps. Moments later, Dionna emerges from the bathroom butt naked. I bend her over on the couch and start eating her from the back. Next, I insert myself in her and pump her from the back. We make love on the couch on and off several times while Jen sleeps on the bed.

We finish having sex and watch some television. After watching several shows, Jen wakes up and walks into the living room. Dionna and I decide to still take her to Chucky Cheese even though it's getting dark. Dionna tightens up Jen's hair up and we drive over to the spot. We walk Jen inside and she goes crazy. It's as if the lights have sent an electric current through her body. She's running around nonstop from game to game. She even makes some friends. They're playing tag and other kiddie games. A couple hours later, I decide it's time to eat.

"Babe, do me a favor. I need you to order a pizza and some drinks from the food court. I'm sure Jen has to be starved by now. I'll let her run around for a little while longer and bring her over when the food comes out," I say.

"K, what you want on the pizza? And what you want to drink?" Dionna asks.

"Just get pepperoni on it. Get her whatever kinda juice they got and get me a sprite," I answer.

I reach in my pocket and hand Dionna a fifty-dollar bill. She walks over to the food court and gets on the line. Jen is running around as happy as can be. I interrupt Jen's fun when I take her to the picture booth. We take several pictures and wait for the machine to dispense them. I turn around and look at Dionna when I hear her call my name. I see she's carrying the soft drinks to a table and one of the Chucky Cheese employees is following her with the pizza. Finally, the pictures dispense, so I grab them. I look at them as Jen and I walk over to the table.

We start eating the pizza and Dionna looks at the pictures. She compliments me on how good I look with my niece and assures me that I'm going to make a great father someday. I don't doubt that I'd make a great father because I know I would. However, I can't be a good dad if I'm out here peddling drugs across the state. Well, I'm in knee deep for now and I'm not planning to have any children anytime soon. I wonder if Dionna is trying to hint to me that she's pregnant. That's the second time in the last few hours that she's mentioned me and fatherhood.

"You keep telling me about me and kids. It seems like you're hinting at something to me. You know you don't have to beat around the bush with me. You can tell me straight-forwardly. Don't drag your feet," I articulate.

"Umm, you know I don't sugarcoat a damn thing, so stop it and if I was pregnant, I wouldn't drop hints, I'd just tell you outright. So, no, I'm not pregnant," Dionna utters.

"Okay, that's real. I know you tell it like it is. Always have, since we met. My bad on that. I'm bugging," I state apologetically.

"Yeah, you were off your rocker with that one. Get your head back in the game," Dionna says.

"That's too easy. I won't even touch that one. That's like a wide-open layup," I tell Dionna as I laugh.

"I'm sure that was Mr. Mind Always in the Gutter," she remarks.

We talk a little longer while we eat. We finish eating and head to the car. Dionna straps Jen in the car seat. Unfortunately, Jen is a little unsettled for some unknown reason to us, so Dionna rides in the backseat with her. I listen to how compassionate Dionna is with Jen as I drive the car. While I'm driving, my brother calls me and asks me to drop Jen off at her grandmother's house, which is right by the park. I agree to take her to Linden even though it's out of the way.

Twenty minutes later, we pull up to Jen's

grandmother's house. I get out the car and go to the backseat to pull Jen out of the car. I pull her out of the car at the same time Dionna is opening the back door on her side. As I pull Jen out of the car, I clumsily drag her foot and her shoe comes off. I ask Dionna to grab her shoe. Dionna leans down to pick her shoe up. Simultaneously, I hear an engine roar and then car tires screech piercingly. Next, several shots ring out and disturb the quiet of the night. I turn my body to cover Jen and fall to the ground. My back windshield completely shatters and glass is thrown everywhere.

I reach in my waist and grab my gun. Dionna is screaming out of control. My niece is crying an ominous cry. I'm waiting for the gunfire to stop or for me to hear a car door open before I pop my head up and start returning fire. Fortunately, the gunfire stops, the car pulls off and zooms wildly down Essex Ave. I peek my head up and see the car. I have a clear look at it. I look down at my niece as she's clutched in my arms. Simultaneously, I wonder if Dionna is okay.

"D, you good? D, did you get shot?" I ask while screaming at the top of my lungs.

I hold Jen tightly and run around to the other side of the car to check on Dionna. She hasn't answered me yes, but is still screaming out of control. I don't know if she's been shot and is screaming because of the pain she's in or because she's too shook to speak. I damn sure hope it's the latter. I open the door and Dionna is still crouched down in the backseat. Surprisingly, she's still holding my niece's shoe. I don't see any blood on her even though she's covered in glass from my windshield breaking. I sit Jen down and help Dionna out the car.

"Yo, you good? Did you get hit?" I ask.

"I...I'm good... I think I'm good," Dionna answers in a shaken tone.

"Get up! Let me look at you and make sure you good," I say.

I walk Dionna to the grass patch on the sidewalk. She crouches down next to my niece. They're both visibly shaken. I'm sure my niece was just startled by the loud gunfire interrupting her sleep. She'll be fine in a few minutes, I'm sure. However, Dionna knows what happened. I wonder if she'll think it was random or if she'll blame me. Either way it goes, I ain't copping to nothing. I'll play it like I don't know what happened and maybe it was a case of mistaken identity.

I wrap my arms around the both of them. My adrenaline is pumping at a maximum level, but I'm not shook. I'm actually very calm. I know I need to be calm for my niece and Dionna. I never show weakness in front of anyone especially my woman. I rub Dionna's back as she rests her head on my shoulder.

"It's gonna be alright. You just need to calm down. I don't know what the heck that was about," I say. "I'm just glad we're all okay."

"Yeah, me too. That was crazy. I can't even front. I thought my life was over. I saw my life flash before my eyes," Dionna tells.

"Damn, Babe. I don't even know what to say. I'm glad your life didn't end and that you're still here with me," I comment.

"Me too," Dionna speaks while sobbing.

Jen's grandmother heard the gunfire and is running outside in a panic. She's screaming and asking us if we're alright. Jen's grandmother immediately grabs Jen out of my embrace. She looks Jen up and down to ensure that she's fine. I grab my niece's shoe out of Dionna's hand and put it on Jen's foot. I take her car seat and bag out of my car and put it on the porch. Jen's grandmother takes her inside.

"Come on Babe. We gotta go," I voice.

"Go where? You not gonna call the cops?" Dionna asks in a surprised tone.

"Nah, I ain't even trying to fool with the cops like that. Somehow or another it'll be my fault and they'll lock me up. Besides, they aren't gonna do anything. We'll be jammed up for hours at the station and it'll all be a waste of time," I dictate.

Dionna agrees with my response. It's actually true that they won't do anything. I'm not giving a description of the car, so they'll have nothing to go off of. All it'll be is paperwork. I really need to call AK to tell him what happened, but I can't with Dionna in the car. AK is going to fly off the deep end and Dionna can't hear that conversation. Plus, I won't be able to talk to him the way I want to. Normally, the journey back to Dionna's dorm is quick, but tonight is different. I guess I feel this way because I really want to drop her off and get to kick it with AK. We finally make it to Dionna's dorm. I walk her to her dorm from the parking lot. She informs me that she's okay.

"Good night, I'll hit you in the morning," I say as I kiss her on the cheek.

"K, good night love," Dionna replies.

# CHAPTER 10

I walk back to my car and call AK, but he doesn't answer the phone. Damn, I really need this guy to answer the phone. I have to put him on to what happened tonight. He's definitely going to flip his wig. I know I wanted to chase that car down and shoot it up. I'm livid ten times over. That nigga Gary tried to kill me and that's cool to some degree. I'm a part of the game, so I expect to have my life in jeopardy, but my family and lady are off limits because they aren't involved in this life. Gary should know that. There are rules to this shit and he's should abide by them. Since he violated, I must violate him. He's as good as dead in my eyes.

I've called AK several times, but he hasn't answered or replied. Oh shit, what if he's not answering because Gary shot at him and was able to kill him. That'll be wild as hell if AK is dead.

I'm really going to go on a rampage if that's the case. I dial his number again, but the result is the same. He doesn't answer. Do I want to ride out solo or just wait to hear back from AK? Man, I have to put an end to this tonight. If I wait, Gary may be expecting it. On the other hand, if I go to his crib now, I can probably catch him slipping. That's the move. I'm out.

I get on Park Ave. in Linden to head to the Turnpike when my phone starts ringing. It's AK calling. I grab the phone and answer the call like my life depended on it.

"Yo, nigga! Where you at?" I ask urgently.

"Damn, nigga. You clocking me like you my bitch or something," he replies jokingly. "I just got the draws from that freak I met at da club last week."

"Son, we gotta get up ASAP. Like right now," I say sternly.

"Why my nigga? What's good?" AK asks urgently.

"I got shot at, but I ain't really trying to do all this talking over the phone. Meet me at the park, so I can put you on," I order.

AK voices, "Nigga, tell me you playing! Yo, I'm on Michigan Ave. right off 22. I'll be at the park in like 15 minutes."

"Aight, I'm here!" I yell.

A few minutes later, AK pulls up. He jumps out the car quickly with an intense scowl on his face. I explain to him the entire scenario of what happened with the shooting. He is very upset that someone tried to kill me and had the gumption to shoot at me with my niece and Dionna with me.

"Yo, you think it was Gary?" he asks.

"Nah, I don't think it was that nigga! I know it was him," I answer as I punch my fist into my other hand.

"It had to be him, but how you know it was him? You saw his face or something?" AK inquires.

"Son, I got a look at the car when it sped away. But peep this, it's not the car that's normally in the garage when we go to pick up the shit. He has a gray Integra that he never drives. I saw it parked on the street one time. Now, I've never seen him drive it, but I'm sure it's the same whip," I communicate.

"My nigga you ain't got to say no more. Even if it wasn't him, he had somebody do it. Me and you been in this drug shit for a couple years now and never had no beef. Then all of a sudden you get shot at while we beefing with Gary. Nigga he did it and we gonna put that nigga down. Fuck it! It's either him or us!" AK articulates angrily.

"Son, I'm trying to hit this nigga crib right fuckin now. That mother fucker gotta go!" I verbalize frankly.

"Nigga let's go!" AK says.

"We gotta find a whip to take. You see my shit all beat up and we can't take yours because it's too risky. We can't let ya whip be seen," I word.

He utters, "Oh no doubt! Yo, I got the keys to a fiend's whip. That shit is parked by the tracks. We can take that shit and ride down to old boy's house and put that work in."

"Hell yeah! That's the fuckin move then!" I voice adamantly.

"Yo, grab that blanket from out ya whip," AK orders.

The tracks are only a few blocks from the park, so we can walk over there. As AK said, the fiend's car is parked right by the tracks. Sometimes he'll drive a fiend's car if he has to drop something off or if the fiend wants a couple of dollars. We jump in the car and head for the Turnpike. AK is driving and is covered up in an attempt to keep the camera from seeing his face. I'm in the back seat of the car with the blanket completely over me. Nobody can tell that I'm in the car.

"Yo, we pushing this nigga wig back on sight! That nigga's last breath is gonna be tonight!" AK boasts.

"Son, he don't even know what it is! I'm not doing no talking. I'm just shooting. Fuck dat nigga," I remark.

AK mentions, "Yo, dude might have some cash in the crib. We might be able to rob his ass too. Straight rob his ass and then kill him. That's the type shit that I'm on."

"Son, that's the type shit that we need to be on! I'm with it. Might as well get some paper before we off that bitch ass nigga," I verbalize. "Yo, if nothing else, we gonna scoop the work I hid in his garage."

"Hell yeah! All I'm saying is that we coming outta that bitch with whateva he got in there. Nigga, we bout to come off crazy!" AK boasts.

We zip down the Turnpike and make it to Gary's crib in no time. We park the car on the street and see the grey Integra parked in Gary's yard off to the side. I'm positive that this is the car that pulled down Essex after the shooting. I'm ready for war. I'll feel no guilt after we off Gary because he brought this on himself. We creep across the grass and make it to the side of Gary's house undetected. We walk around the house looking for a way in, but we don't find one. We see Gary sitting on the couch in the living room. Gary looks at his phone screen and answers it then he gets up and walks out our line of sight. AK moves to another window to see if he can see what Gary is doing. A moment later, AK returns to the window I'm at and Gary returns to the living room and sits on the couch while he talks on the phone. Our emotions are raging like angry bulls.

"Did you see him?" I ask.

AK answers, "Yeah, I saw him. He went in the other room and was doing some shit in the floorboards, but I couldn't see what because his body was shielding my line of sight."

"Damn, son, we gotta get in the crib! Ain't no way we gonna get him if we can't get in the house," I say.

"Hell yeah! I'm thinking the same shit you thinking. Son, I'm down to shoot through the mother fucking window right now to murk his ass. I don't even give a fuck," AK reveals wildly.

"Son, I want to body this nigga just as bad as you, but that's some reckless shit you talking about right now. We gotta be smarter than that. If we shoot through the glass, the entire neighborhood will hear it. They'll call the cops and they'll swarm on us like flies on a dead body. To top it all off, we may not even hit the nigga through the window," I explain rationally.

"That's real shit. Well that nigga gotta stop breathing tonight, so we gotta figure it out," AK announces.

"Yo, stay here and watch the nigga. I'm gonna check something real quick," I say.

I run around to the front of the house where the Integra is parked at. I look inside and see that there's a garage door opener clipped to the sun visor. I know that's our way in. I think it's a bad idea, but many people leave their garage door opener in the car overnight. That's like the dumbest thing in the world. You're basically giving someone access to your crib. I go get AK and tell him about the garage door opener.

"Aight, so we break in the car and hit the

garage door opener. While the door is lifting up, we gotta be rolling under the door and moving. We can't waste no time," AK says.

I voice, "I feel you. We gotta be on our shit for real. He gonna let off a few shots most likely, so be careful."

"We gonna need the door that leads to the house to be unlocked, so we'll be able to slide right in," AK says.

"Man listen, it ain't no way that door is locked. I've never been to anybody's crib and the door leading to the house from the garage been locked. Ain't no way," I word.

"Well, we about to find out," AK responds.

We break into the car and grab the garage door opener. We run back around to the side of the house and look in the window again. We want to know exactly where he's at before we go inside. Fortunately, Gary is still on the couch and is on the phone. We walk over to the garage door and crouch down. I hit the button on the garage door opener and it glides up smoothly. It's barely making any noise. I press the button to stop the door from completely opening. I don't want to take the chance of the door making more noise than necessary and alerting Gary to our presence. The door is open enough for AK and me to slide under it, so I hit the button to stop it. We crouch down and go in the garage. We move slowly through the darkened garage until we make it to the door that leads into the house.

I try to turn the handle to the door and it turns. I push the door open slowly as to not make any noise. We both enter the crib moving slowly, quietly, and meticulously. We hear the television playing in another room. We creep toward the sound of the television and stop outside the living room. I point to AK to cover me and I say a silent prayer. AK and I flash into the living room and look at the couch, but Gary isn't on the couch.

We look at each other with sheer befuddlement. He was just on the couch talking on the phone. I hope he didn't hear the garage door open and go grab his gat. He may have the jump on us. AK and I duck down just in case. I get behind the sofa and AK ducks down on the side of the love seat near the fireplace. I make eye contact with AK and mouth to him that we need to find Gary as soon as possible. AK nods his head in agreement. AK looks around and then suddenly pops up out of his hiding place. He points at the fireplace mantel and is moving towards it. As he reaches for the mantel, Gary appears in the doorway.

"Yo Rah, look at this," AK whispers.

"Who da fuck are you nigga?" Gary questions as he pulls his gun from his waist.

When Gary yells at AK it catches him off guard. He is in no position to fire at Gary because he's fixated on the fireplace mantel. AK turns toward the sound of Gary's voice and freezes like a deer in headlights. Gary raises his gun, points it at AK, and then all you hear is several shots being fired. There's a loud thud as the body falls to the floor. Blood and guts are everywhere. I'm dumbfounded while I'm looking at the seemingly lifeless body on the floor.

"Take that motherfucker! I knew your ass wasn't making it out of the night!" I boast as I move towards his body.

AK states sincerely, "Son, that nigga was about to body me for real. Like with no hesitation. Good looks on having my back on that. I got caught slipping like a mother fucker."

"You already know my nigga. I wasn't bout to let nothing happen to you. I got ya back forever," I say.

"That nigga Gary is dead than a mother fucker. Rat ass nigga!" AK remarks.

"Damn sure is. Yo, but he definitely caught you slipping. You was bugging on that one," I mention.

"Hell yeah, I was, but my attention was caught when I saw the picture on the fireplace mantel. Son, go look at that shit! I don't think I'm bugging. You tell me," AK orates in a concerned tone.

"What da hell is on the mantel?" I ask.

"Son, just go see what I'm talking about and you tell me," AK dictates.

I walk over to the mantel and look for what AK is talking about. I see several pictures and then I see exactly what caught his attention. I pick up one of the pictures and I'm shocked as I examine it. I sit on the arm of the couch in bewilderment.

"So, I guess it's what I was thinking," AK voices as he puts his hand on my shoulder.

"Hell yeah, it is! Fuck!" I scream angrily.

"Son, I know you mad, but we got to get the fuck outta here right now. But before we go, I gotta run in that back room. I saw Gary go in there and drop something in the floorboard when I looked through the window," AK reports.

He dips out of the living room and comes back with a bag of cash. I'm still sitting on the arm of the couch. I don't even get excited when I see him with all that cash. AK takes the picture out of my hand and places it back on the mantel. He grabs me by the arm and pulls me toward the garage. Seconds later, I snap out of my daze and realize the urgency of us getting out of here. AK and I enter the garage. I zoom to the spot where I hid the drugs and am delighted to find them right where I left them. I snatch the drugs and we roll under the door from which we entered. I hit the garage door button and the door closes shut. As we run away from the house, I throw the garage door opener back in the car.

AK and I make it back to the car undetected. We drive off the block and disappear into the darkness. We make it back to the Turnpike and cruise past each exit. AK and I take the gun that

I killed Gary with and throw it in the Arthur Kill in Elizabeth along with the burner phone Gary called us on. Fortunately, AK had the presence of mind to take the burner phone. Next, we go back to Linden and drop the fiend's car off by the tracks. After that, we walk back to the park and sit on the bleachers. AK rolls a blunt and lights it up.

"Son, I ain't gonna front. That shit got me twisted! And what's crazy is that when I asked her if she had any siblings, she said yeah. Then she told me her brother was stationed in Hawaii and that he's in the military," I explain.

AK words, as he smokes a blunt, "I feel you fam. That shit had me froze for a second too. Yeah, I remember when you told me that he was a military nigga, but all these bitches lie fam."

"I guess you right, but damn yo. I should've peeped this. I can't believe that Gary is Dionna's brother Derek. That's some wild shit. The fucking family photo and his high school graduation picture just sitting there in plain sight," I voice.

"Yo, it ain't ya fault though. Gary was using fake names with us just like we were using fake names with him. Gary knew what time it was and we were only doing what we had to do to protect ourselves," AK assures.

"Yeah, I know it wasn't no other way, but I just know Dionna gonna be fucked up over this. And it's gonna be all my fault. Son, if I would've known that Gary was her brother, we would've worked something out. Ain't no way that nigga is the police," I convey.

AK verbalizes in a matter-of-fact tone, "But that's not what happened my nigga. And if he wasn't da police, it would've been impossible for him to find out that we from Linden. The whole time we were telling him that we from Irvington.

I respond, "I know it aint, but damn. I just wish I would've known Gary and Derek was the same person then I would've moved differently or something."

AK takes a pull of the blunt and utters, "I feel you, but he shot at you, ya niece, and Dionna. That nigga had to die. Stop babbling. We handled our biz based on the info we had at that time."

"That's what's even more fucked up. If he would've known Dionna was with me, he would've never opened fire and would've been more inclined for us to work it out. Damn, this shit is ill!"

AK trying to be the voice of reason explains, "It ain't nearly as ill as it could've gotten. What could've happened is that me, you, ya girl, and your niece could all be dead from fucking around with Gary's bitch ass. Stop stressing over that shit. Bottom line is that it was either him or us and I'm happy than a mother fucker that it was him."

"Word. That's one hunnett. It is much better

that it's him. Good looking out my nigga. Let me get the fuck outta here. I got to get a few hours of sleep before work tomorrow," I say as I get up from the bleachers.

"Aight, yo you good?" AK asks.

"Yeah fam. I'm straight. Just gonna wait for Dionna to hit me up about her brother and console her. I know she's gonna be finished," I answer.

"That's what it is. But, now I know you ain't good," AK charges.

"Why you say that?" I inquire.

"Cause you ain't even trying to get your cut of the money we stole from Gary's crib," he tells.

"Son, you know when it comes to money between you and me that shit ain't serious like that. We'll meet up tomorrow. I gotta work at seven thirty and then class from like twelve to three," I report.

"Aight, hit me up! I ain't gonna be doin shit," AK words.

"I got you son. Imma hit you when I'm leaving campus," I verbalize.

"Aight, my nigga, but one other thing before you bounce," AK words.

"Word. I'm listening," I state as I'm opening my car door.

"If Gary or Derek or whateva that dead nigga's name is, was the police, the police will def be comin to pay us a visit," AK verbalizes.

"Put me on my nigga," I say.

AK explains, "Well, if he was the police then they know about us since they were working with him, which is what made them pull us over."

"Hell yeah! You right about that. If that's the case, they'll be coming for us once they find out Gary's a dead man," I say.

"You already know, so we can't move no product for a minute because we don't want them to run down on us and we have drugs in the whip," AK articulates.

I shoot back, "Hell yeah! Or even worse, they follow us for a while and see all the spots we move work to and lock every fuckin body up."

"That's real shit my nigga. Good thing is we can afford to lay low for a minute until we see where this thing goes," AK expresses.

I enunciate, "Well, since we're polyin this shit, I'm trippin on the fact that Gary tried to kill me."

"I don't get why you're trippin. The nigga was mad over the shit and wanted revenge. Simple shit," AK chimes in.

I blurt, "But nah. It ain't so simple. Peep where I'm goin with this. This nigga is the police, but tries to kill me. That doesn't make much sense to me."

AK admits, "Oh shit my nigga! You right! A nigga workin for the cops ain't shootin up da block up. Fuck!"

"That's what I'm saying! If he was the cops, he wouldn't risk a murder charge," I suggest.

AK reveals, "I think you were right when you

said ain't no way he was the police. That was our bad, but he still did try to kill you. I still don't regret doing what we did."

"I ain't mad how it turned out either. I guess the cops really just saw our whips driving back and forth and thought it was suspicious. What a fuckin coincidence," I phrase.

"It was, but handle ya handle and get at me later," AK remarks.

I jump in the whip and pull off. I forgot that my damn window is shot the fuck out. I gotta go get this joint fixed after class. I drive to the crib and switch clothes. I walk down my steps leading to the backyard while carrying the clothes we wore to kill Gary. I set them on fire in the backyard and go back upstairs. After that, I take a shower and go to sleep.

# CHAPTER 11

Morning rolls around way too fast. I only got a few hours of sleep and to make matters worse, my sleep wasn't the best to say the least. Last night's activities are really messing with my head. I'm not the type to ever let anyone see me sweat. I have to shake this shit off. I get out the bed and freshen up. Next, I grab a banana and a bottle of water. It's time for me to go to work, so I jump in the car and head to the airport. My music is on full blast as I drive down Irvine Turner. My phone starts vibrating on my hip.

"Good morning, Babe? How you?" I ask after I answer the phone.

"Hey, morning," Dionna says in a sullen tone.

I ask, "Is everything alright? Is something bothering you?"

"No, nothing is bothering me. Everything is

alright, I guess. I'm probably just tripping over nothing," Dionna speaks.

"If you have to guess that everything is alright, then most likely something is wrong. You might as well tell me what may or may not be a problem. I know it can't be with me because I didn't do anything," I say calmly.

"My bad. You haven't done anything to me. I don't mean to be standoffish, but I'm kinda worried about my peeps," Dionna tells.

"You don't have to apologize to me. I can be a little iffy when something's on my mind too. Why you worried about your peeps?" I inquire.

"Cause my peeps haven't called me back since last night and that never happens. I always get a call back even if it's in the morning," she answers.

I chuckle as I voice, "Maybe ya peeps fell asleep or just straight up forgot or something. Ya peeps' battery could've died. I'm sure over the years there's been times when you didn't get a call back."

"Thanks Ray, I know you're trying to make me feel better and I appreciate it. I really do, but I think something's really wrong," she conveys.

"Honey, why you think that?" I ask.

"For one, I was on the phone with him last night and while we were talking, he told me that he heard a noise. He said he thought it was the garage opening up, but then it stopped like all of a sudden. He figured he was tripping, but he got off the phone with me to check it out. He said he holla back in a second, but never did. That's when I started getting worried," Dionna explains as she starts crying.

Damn, this is crazy as hell. It was Dionna who Gary was on the phone with when we got to his crib. The timing on that is unbelievable. If he hadn't told her he'd call her back, she would've heard the entire murder. That would've really devastated her. I wonder if Dionna can hear the guilt in my voice. I try to sound as normal as possible. I don't want to say anything unlike myself and make Dionna suspicious.

"Don't cry baby. Well maybe he was just playing a bad joke on you. I know you told him about us getting shot at," I orate.

"That's why I called him, but as soon as he picked up the phone, he heard the noise and said he'd call me back," Dionna communicates.

"Hmm, I don't want to make you more nervous, but that does sound a little suspicious. You know I'm not the scary type, but something seems a little off. I'm sure you've called him mad times after that," I utter.

"See, I knew I wasn't crazy for feeling the way I'm feeling. I even called my mom and aunt to tell them and they both said I was tripping. I think they really just rushed me off the phone because they're in Vegas partying and didn't want me to interrupt them any further," Dionna articulates. "And you know I was blowing his phone up all night."

"Damn D. I hope he's good. I'm saying, I think you should call the cops and have them do a welfare check or something," I say.

"Umm, hell no! I'm not sending the police to his house. They might kill him. You know how the cops do. Plus, he'd curse me out if I sent them there," Dionna remarks in a peeved tone.

"Hell yeah, I can see that going the wrong way. My bad on that. Well, ask a neighbor to slide through real quick," I suggest.

"No, he don't fool with them like that either because he keeps to himself. Plus, I don't got his neighbor's number anyway," Dionna explains.

"You know I feel him on that. I'm not one to fool with people I don't know like that either," I state.

My mind is racing a thousand miles per second right now. Dionna doesn't want to call the cops and she doesn't want the neighbors over at his crib. Why is that? Is it really because she doesn't trust the police? I wonder if she knows about her brother's drug enterprise and is not as innocent as she plays to be. Maybe Dionna doesn't want the police at his crib because she doesn't want her brother to end up in jail. For that matter, maybe she knows about me and is okay with it. I have to feel her out a little more.

"So, what's your plan to ease your mind? You know you can't carry that stress all day, right?" I ask.

"Yeah, I know I can't. I think my only option is to drive back home and hit his crib and see what's good for myself," Dionna answers.

I respond, "That's what it is. You should go. It'll ease your mind. He'll probably be chilling with some broad when you get there."

"I hope you're right," she says.

"Word up. Me too," I shoot back.

"Feel free to jump in the car with me. I always love your company Babe," she voices warmly.

"Shoot, you know I'm always down, but it depends on what time you going. I'm heading to work now and then I got class after that. Then I wanted to take my car to get the window fixed," I report.

"Oh, I'm sorry Babe. I'm thinking about myself and forgot about you had to handle your business. Don't even worry about it. I'll be fine. I was just being needy," she words.

"Aight, well if you good, I'm gonna holla back later. I'm almost at work anyway," I say.

"K, big head. Thanks for listening to my concerns," she states.

"Come on now. You know you don't got to thank me. That's what I'm here for," I reply.

I put the phone down and turn my music back up. Maybe I can listen to one more full song before I have to get out the whip and catch the shuttle to the building. As soon as I start playing Quiet Storm Remix, my phone starts ringing and vibrating. I look down at the screen and see that is AK calling. I answer the call.

"Yo, what's good?" I ask as I turn the music down.

"Shit. Yo, you by yourself?" he asks.

"Yeah, why what's going on?" I inquire.

"Yo, tell me you found one of your black gloves. Son, when I went to burn all the clothes I had on, the fucking glove was missing!" AK reports urgently.

"My nigga say word! Hell no, I haven't seen the glove. I hope that shit is in the fiend's car. If not, it's most likely still in the fucking house!" I say madly.

"That's what the fuck I was thinking, so I drove to Linden to check the car. I'm in Linden now. I just searched the entire car and ain't see shit yo," AK verbalizes.

"Yo, what the fuck nigga! You bugging! That glove got my DNA and yours on it for sure. If the cops find that glove, they'll have evidence against us to build a case," I report angrily.

"Nigga, calm down. They don't have our DNA on file to match it to. We good as long as we never have to give up our DNA for anything," AK speaks casually.

I shoot back, "Nah, nigga you buggin! Ain't no way I want to live with that possibility over my head. And besides that, Dionna bought me those gloves, so if she sees it, we're fucked. She'll know I was there. Nigga, or if the cops find it and ask her about it, we're fucked because you know she'll identify the glove as being mine. It won't be long before they come for you after they get me."

"Shit! This shit is fucked up nigga. Damn, I slipped up! Fuck it! I just gotta go there and get the glove out the house then. Don't nobody know that he's dead yet, so I'll get the garage door opener and go back in," AK vocalizes.

"Well my nigga, that may not be entirely true," I reply quickly.

AK asks immediately, "Why you say that fam?"

"Yo, as luck would have it Dionna was on the phone with the nigga when we ran up in the spot," I voice.

AK shoots back, "Yo, get the fuck outta here. Damn, she heard the whole shit. That's crazy!"

"Nah, but she almost did. She said he ended the call when he heard a noise," I respond.

AK verbalizes, "That's good shit because she definitely didn't need to hear he hammer ring. Shit nigga, I'm still going down there though. Fuck the bull shit!"

I state rationally, "Yo, if you go down there during the day, someone is bound to peep you. They may call the cops and then it's a done deal. You'd be caught in the vicinity of a dead body then the glove links you to the house. We'd still end up in jail forever."

"Damn, so what the fuck we gonna do? This shit could get ugly fast as hell. It might be time to leave Jersey or even the country. We got paper and fake ids. Nigga, I'm not perishing in no fucking cage. Hell no! I'm better than that," AK articulates.

"Wait, nigga. We might not have to do none of that. I'm about to check something out. I gotta go right now. Imma hit you in a few. If I get it off, we'll be golden. Holla," I state enthusiastically.

"Nigga, hit me up. Later," AK replies.

I dump the call and immediately call Dionna back. She answers the phone and is surprised to hear back from me so soon. I know she's surprised to hear from me because I should be at the job by now. Instead, I'm headed to Montclair State to pick Dionna up, but she doesn't know it yet. I know my window of opportunity to get that glove out of the crime scene is slimmer than the point of a safety pin. If Dionna goes home alone and sees what AK and I have done, she'll call the cops immediately. After that, all it would take is for some cops to be diligent and my life as a free man would be over.

"I know you're surprised to hear from me, but I'm headed your way. I know you're kinda worried and emotional and I think I need to be with you right now," I narrate.

"Oh my goodness! That's so sweet Babe! I know you not serious. You ain't gotta come all the way out here now. You're gonna get in trouble for missing a day," Dionna speaks.

I respond, "I know I don't have to, but I want to. I'll be alright with work. I'll just take a personal day. My shift doesn't start for a few more minutes, so I'll just call them when we hang up."

"Awe, look at my man having my back, but are you sure?" she asks.

"Oh yeah. I always got my Babe's back. But yeah, I'm sure. It'll all be fine. That's what personal days are for. This is an emergency situation in my book," I declare firmly.

I really want Dionna to mention riding down to her brother's house to check on things. Nothing else really matters at this point. My life of freedom is potentially hanging in the balance. Hell, not just mine, AK's life as he knows it hinges on me retrieving that glove before anyone else does. I'm sure we'd be looking at life in prison if we get caught.

Dionna is talking about everything other than what I want to hear. All I want her to say is for me to drive her to south Jersey. Why is she not mentioning it? Dionna is beating me in my head about one of her roommates not cleaning the sink after she left her hair in it. Who really gives a fuck? I know I don't. This shit is killing me. One minute she was consumed with worry about her brother and then the next minute she's worried about minutia. I shouldn't be surprised because this is just how she operates.

"Yo, I'm thinking that you could meet me at the window place, so I don't gotta wait up there all damn day," I make known.

I really do need to drop my car off, but the main reason I brought it up was because I wanted to change the subject to handling business. I'm figuring Dionna will have to mention going to check on her brother again. If she doesn't, I'm just going to bring it up again. I'll play like I'm truly concerned about her brother and her peace of mind.

"We can do that. Well, since you're gonna miss work to make sure I'm good, I'll miss class to take you to the shop," Dionna expresses.

"Bet, that's what it is! I kinda feel like we're using the old school barter system. I give you grapes and you give me apples," I voice.

"Boy, you know you stupid," she says as she laughs.

"I have always been silly. Just wanna make you laugh," I reveal.

"Don't I know it? Where's the shop at?" Dionna asks.

"It's in Linden on St. George's Ave. Right over the bridge where the gas station is. We stopped there before when I had that flat," I disclose.

"Oh yeah. I remember that spot. Wait, for that matter you might as well just head there and I'll meet you out in Linden at the shop. It doesn't make sense for you to drive way out here and then turn around to go right back out there. Just for us to turn right back around and head to campus," Dionna imparts eloquently.

"No doubt. Makes perfect sense. Then let's do that. I'll head to the shop and you'll be on the way," I note.

"K, I'm leaving campus now. By the way, I think we should go to my hometown to check on things, if you're good with that," Dionna insists.

"True, I'm wit it. I was gonna say something about it, but I didn't know if you still wanted to take that ride," I communicate.

"Yeah, I do. Won't be right until I hear from him," Dionna assures.

"Aight, well I'm down to roll," I notify.

If she won't be right until she hears from him, she ain't never going to be right. Shit, maybe she'll see him on the other side. It's a real weird feeling when you know something that's this life altering and the other person doesn't know anything about it. I wonder if I've ever been on the side of the unknown. I guess it doesn't really matter because I wouldn't have known what they knew anyway. Dionna tells me that she'll meet me at the shop and we get off the phone.

I get off one and nine on Haynes Ave. so I can bust a U-turn and head to Linden. My mind is in doing summersaults. I'm physically driving down the highway, but my mind is not with me.

My thoughts are in Cherry Hill and finding that glove. I hope this glove doesn't turn out in the courtroom like I'm OJ Simpson or something. I have the music blasting as loud as it can go, but it's still not drowning out my thoughts. Where the fuck is that glove? Is it in the living room, the garage, or in the backyard? Ain't no telling where the fucking glove is.

I make it to the shop and walk inside. I talk to the attendant and he gets me checked in. They tell me that it'll take three hours for them to replace my back windshield. I'm cool with that because I know that we won't be back from Cherry Hill by then. Once we find the body and call the cops, we'll most likely be there for several hours. I'm sure they'll question us to death. I definitely won't be making it to campus to go to class.

A little while later, Dionna pulls up. She sees me sitting with my back to the glass, but doesn't know I already spotted her. She jumps out the car and comes into the shop and tries to grab me. Instead of her grabbing me, I grab her. I hold her tight and she holds me tighter. What was meant to be a joke turns into a warm and tight embrace that she clearly needs. I kiss her on her nose and then she buries her head on my chest. I hold her in my arms and walk her to the car. I open the passenger's side door and Dionna sits down. I jump in the driver's seat and we pull off.

"I like your little work uniform. You always

look cute in it," Dionna informs as she rubs my thigh.

"That's what it is. You know you always look good as hell no matter what you put on," I compliment. "I know one thing and that is you better stop rubbing my leg like that before big beef stands up."

"I know I do. Thank you very much. I ain't following you up Mr. Big Beef. Maybe medium beef," Dionna cracks.

We hit the highway and are cruising. Dionna is yapping about stuff on campus. I think she's making small talk just to keep from worrying herself to death. I'm listening to her ramble, but I'm not focused on her. I'm even telling her jokes to keep her laughing, but it's all a dog and pony show. I drive straight to the exit for Gary's crib without even thinking. I see her cut her eye at me. I know she's wondering how I know what exit he lives off of.

"Let me find out," she says.

"What's that Babe?" I ask while playing dumb.

"Let me find out you know where you going is what I'm talking about," she answers.

"D, you are really shot the fuck out," I shoot back to her while pretending to laugh.

The truth of the matter is that I would've driven straight to Gary's house if I didn't see her look at me with confusion all in her face. My mind is so focused on getting to the house and finding that glove that I totally forgot that I supposedly have never been to his crib. I would've never been able to reasonably explain how I knew that. I don't know what lie I could've told her to justify driving to his front door. I dodged a bullet for real.

"Umm, no I'm serious. You damn near at his crib," she insists.

"Well, you know I have a little bit of psychic in me. Nah, for real though. You buggin out. I came this way because this is the way to your crib, so I figured it had to be close," I explain.

"Damn, that makes sense. My mind is all over the place. I wasn't even thinking about none of that," she phrases.

I convey, "I know you not thinking right. It's okay. I love you anyway. Even though you're crazy as hell."

"Boy, I ain't crazy. I just had a brain freeze. Don't act like you don't have them from time to time," Dionna claims.

We pass the gas station where Dionna works from time to time. I let her know that the rest of the way to his house is on her. She tells me that we're only a few minutes away. I was just here last night, but I can't tell her that. I drive two more miles and Dionna tells me to make a left at the light and I do so. Next, she tells me to make a slight left. Before long, we're on the block. I decide to further my charade.

"Damn, yo! Your peeps is living good as hell

out here! What the fuck!" I state pretending to be shocked.

"Yeah, but he didn't always live out here. He used to live in Camden in the projects, but that all changed," she discloses.

"Wow, that's crazy! He had one hell of a come up! That's like some rags to riches shit," I voice.

"Yeah, he definitely came up. He actually won a lawsuit that really turned things around for him. He had nerve damage and they paid him for that, but he fully recovered. You wouldn't be able to tell by looking at him. We all and thought he was lying until he got the money," she verbalizes.

"True, I hate that he had to suffer, but he's living damn good now," I offer.

I've never been a dummy in my life. I'd have to be stupid as hell to believe some lawsuit story like that. He most likely told them that story when he started selling weight. He probably knew his mom would know he was a drug dealer if he didn't tell her that story. Dude probably only comes off a little bit of money at a time to really sell them on the story. It really seems like Dionna bought the lies he told.

"I mean it's cool. Like I said, he's like normal just with more money. It did make him a little paranoid. He doesn't want people at the house and doesn't want to meet a lot of new people," she narrates.

"Gotcha," I word.

Dionna tells me that the house with the big columns and all brick is the house. I turn in the driveway and drive up to the garage. I see the Integra is still parked in the same spot it was last night. To my delight, it doesn't look like anyone has been here. Dionna hits her garage door button and starts to get out the car. I grab her by the wrist and point to the Integra.

"It looks like the window is busted. Look at the glass on the ground," I tell.

"Oh, my goodness! It damn sure is!" Dionna says as she sees what I'm seeing.

I only pointed out the glass on the ground to her because I want some time alone in the house, so I can find that glove. Unfortunately, my plan doesn't work. Dionna jumps out the car and goes over to the driver's side window of the Integra. She immediately runs in the garage and I follow her while looking at every inch of the ground and floor for the glove. Sadly, I don't see the glove near the front of the house or in the garage.

Next, I follow Dionna through the garage door that leads directly into the house. I'm waiting for her to call out for Derek, but she doesn't. Instead, she calls out for Dre. I'm totally flabbergasted. I have no clue as to why she's calling for Dre or who Dre he even is. She begins to call the name again, but he's not responding. I hear panic begin to set in Dionna's voice as the calls of Dre's name become more frequent and horror filled. She's ahead of me and clears the hallway that leads to the living room. Next, she lets out the most excruciating wale of pain I've ever heard and takes off running. She falls to the floor over her brother's dead body.

"Oh my God! He's dead! Somebody killed my Dre!" she hollers in agony.

"Oh shit! What the fuck! Yo, you don't need to be in here. You shouldn't be seeing this!" I say sternly.

Dionna weeps over her dead brother's body. She even starts to clutch him. I know she shouldn't be touching his body because she is contaminating the crime scene, but for my intents and purposes I'm all for it. It's even better that I'm in here too. Now if they find my hair follicles or some other incriminating evidence, I'll be covered. This shit is working out to my favor, but I still need to find that damn glove. There would be no way to explain gunshot residue on the glove. I'm still incredibly confused as to why she's calling Gary Dre, instead of Derek.

Dionna buries her head in my chest again, but this time it's different. She is now face to face with the reality that she's dreaded since last night. Something did happen to her brother. I shot him dead in his own home. While I'm embracing Dionna, I scour the room with my eyes to see if I can spot the glove anywhere, but I don't. I tell Dionna that we have to call the police immediately. I know we can't stay in here for too much longer without calling the authorities. Dionna agrees with me, so she breaks free of my embrace and walks over to the phone sitting on the end table and dials 9-1-1.

I walk up behind her and rub her back as she dials. I look to the spot where AK was ducked down on the side of the sofa, but I see no glove. I don't see a damn thing. I still have to check outside to see if he dropped it on the side or the backyard.

"This is 9-1-1 what's your emergency?" the 9-1-1 dispatch says.

"I want to report a homicide," Dionna says in a broken tone.

The 9-1-1 dispatch asks Dionna a series of questions. She tells the dispatch who the victim is and what her name is. I'm burning inside because I still have no clue as to where the glove is and I don't know why she told the dispatch that the victim's name is Andre Miller. Either way, I need to focus on finding the glove. What the fuck am I going to do? I can't just go roaming around the back of the house without arising suspicion. I feel like a fucking sitting duck right now. This is not a good feeling and this is not how I live. Real men take action. I know what I have to do.

"Ma'am it's just me and my boyfriend here. His name is Ray Daniel," Dionna tells.

I have to make sure the 9-1-1 dispatch operator can hear me. I know all of these calls are recorded, so I'll just act like the normal person who calls 9-1-1 in a panic. The operator tells us to leave the house and to go outside and wait for the authorities. I know my only time to act is now, so I seize the opportunity.

I look over at the window and frown my face. Dionna sees my facial expression and is concerned. She asks me what's wrong. I put her behind me, but I don't answer. She asks me the same question, but I don't answer her. I'm really building suspense for the 9-1-1 dispatch. I know at some point she's going to have to ask Dionna what's going on. She's taking a little too long for me to ask, so I'll give her no choice.

"Oh shit, somebody's on the side of the house. I think I just saw somebody looking through the window at us!" I yell out.

I haven't actually seen anyone, but I have to go around the house to see if that glove is back there. There is no other place that shit could be. The 9-1-1 dispatch heard what I said and responds. She asks Dionna if we spotted an unknown person on the premises. Dionna replies that we think someone is running alongside the house.

"If the person is outside, I suggest you find a safe place to hide inside the house. Don't come out until the police arrive. If you can describe what the person looked like and what he or she is wearing, that would be a great help," the dispatch lady conveys.

Simultaneously, I scream out aggressively, "I'm about to catch that nigga. Fuck that. It ain't even going down like that!"

I hear the 9-1-1 dispatch telling Dionna something about me not chasing anyone, but I'm already bolting out of the door by the time she's saying what she's saying. Of course, it's all by design. I know Dionna is genuinely going to flip out about me running after the imaginary criminal. She'll be very sincere as she talks to the 9-1-1 dispatch.

Dionna yells to me, "No, she said don't go after the suspect. You need to hide too. Babe, don't go out there!"

I run out the door and zoom around the side of the house. I'm looking everywhere and I'm getting upset that I haven't seen anything. I hear police sirens getting closer and closer. The multiple blaring sirens inform me that many patrol units are quickly approaching. Each siren is creating an intense panic in my stomach. The bad part is that I don't know if the glove is even on the property. I could be doing all of this for no reason. I make it to the window where AK saw Gary lift up the floorboards. While I'm looking through the window, I see Dionna enter the room.

She's attempting to hide in the room like the 9-1-1 dispatch told her to. I look around the room and see where the floorboards are raised. Next, what I see makes my eyes damn near pop out of their sockets. The fucking glove is on the floor next to the raised floorboards. I guess AK took the glove off his hand to pry the boards up and forgot to put it back on. I hope Dionna doesn't look over there and see the glove. Unfortunately, she hasn't ducked anywhere to hide, so it's possible she may see the glove.

I know she'd recognize that glove in a heartbeat. My heart is beating a thousand pumps a second because Dionna may recognize the glove and because those police sirens are so loud that the police are definitely in the neighborhood. I run back around the side of the house and can see that the units have turned on the block. I have a few more seconds before all of the units have a clear line of sight on the house. If they see me enter the house, they'll probably think that I'm the murderer and lock me up. At a bare minimum, they'll search me and find the glove if I've retrieved it by then.

If they find the glove on me, that'll raise all sorts of suspicions. I can't let them see me. I have to stay low and move swiftly. As I run along the side of the house, I see the front end of a patrol unit. I turn quickly and tightly into the garage and duck down. I crouch down low around Gary's other car parked in the garage and make it to the door that leads inside the house. I ease over to the room that the glove and Dionna are in. At first glance in the room, I don't see Dionna, but I see the glove. I make my way over to the glove and pick it up. I stuff the glove in my nuts and walk over to the closet door.

I call out to Dionna, but she does not respond. I don't know where she is, but I hear the police stampeding into the house. I open the door to the closet that's in the room and get inside. I throw some of the clothes on top of me and just catch my breath. I'm not coming out of here until the police come get me. I won't be on the news for being shot by the police. Moments later, the police enter the room I'm in and call out.

"It's the police, is anyone in here?" One officer asks.

"Yes, I'm in the closet. My name is Ray Daniel. I was one of the people who made the 9-1-1 call," I answer.

I'm looking through the slits in the closet door. I see six officers are in the room. The officers point their guns at the closet door. They're all in uniform and have on bullet proof vests. I know I can't make any sudden moves because they don't know what I could be holding. For all they know, I could be pointing a gun at them from behind the door. Even though they don't know I'm the actual killer, they're proceeding with caution.

"I'm going to need you to exit the closet very slowly. Don't make any sudden moves and follow my instructions. Do you understand?" the officer asks.

"Yes, officer, I understand," I speak.

"I want you to lie flat on your stomach if you can and put your hands behind your head. I know you haven't done anything wrong, but doing this will protect you and us. Let me know when you're on your stomach," the officer states sternly.

"Yes sir. I'm on my stomach and my hands are behind my back," I call out.

"We're going to open the closet door and put you in handcuffs. You're not in any trouble, it's just procedure," he assures.

Seconds later, the closet door swings open. The cops rush in and put me in cuffs. They lift me up and carry me out of the closet. Next, they pat me down to ensure that I don't have any weapons. Of course, I don't have any weapons on me. They walk me out in handcuffs to a patrol unit that's outside. They confirm my story with Dionna and take me out of the handcuffs. The cops ask Dionna and me a series of questions about what we saw when we arrived and what we did. We tell them everything exactly the way it happened.

Dionna told them about what happened when she was on the phone with Dre. The cops wanted to hear every detail about that situation because they feel he heard the person who killed him enter the house. The cops estimate the time of death to be around the time that Dionna talked to him. They have all sorts of people out here. It really looks like an episode of Forensic Files out here. Dionna is really distraught over this. She can't stop crying. I'm consoling her as best as I can. I'm really suffering myself. This internal conflict is killing me. I'm finding it difficult to cope with the fact that I caused the love of my life so much anguish. At the same time, I'm glad I offed him. What I found out from the police questioning is that Gary is really not Derek. It turns out that Dre is her first cousin and was fronting to me and AK like his name was Gary.

The cops see that the window on Gary's Integra is broken and that the garage door opener is on the seat. They ask Dionna if the window was always like that and she informs them that it wasn't. These cops aren't the least bit stupid. They've already surmised that the intruders broke into the car and stole the garage door opener and used it to gain entry into the house. They're right on point with that. I just hope their expertise doesn't put together that AK and I were the ones who did it. They have even ruled out robbery as a motive because they haven't found any items missing from the house.

The officer asks, "Do you know of anyone who would want to harm your cousin? Did he have any enemies or did anyone make threats to him?"

"Not that I know of. I mean even if he did, my cousin wouldn't tell me. He is a private type of person. Plus, I'm a student at Montclair State

University, so I'm not at home a lot. Ain't no telling what he had going on if anything at all," Dionna discusses.

Now, I've never been a snitch in my life and I never will. However, I'm definitely the type of person to take advantage of an opportunity when it falls on my lap. I see no reason why this particular situation would call for me not to do just that. I have the perfect opportunity to ensure that not even the slightest amount of speculation comes my way.

"I understand. I'm not implying anything about your cousin. These types of questions are just routine. We just want to find out who murdered him, so it helps to know who his enemies may be," the officer states.

I say, "We've seen enough crime shows to know that you guys ask a million questions. I ain't mad at you though."

The officer chuckles, "Thanks, well, that's good to know. But yeah, I know all these questions are annoying to a lot of people, but the questions are necessary. They help us solve cases all the time. You guys would be surprised how much seemingly useless information breaks cases wide open. So, any info you can think of, will help tremendously."

"Okay, we'll keep that in mind," Dionna says.

"Be sure to notify your aunt and have her give us a call as soon as possible. She may be able to shed some light on the investigation. I'm sure she spends some time here and will know the happenings of the house," the officer tells.

Dionna words, "I'll be sure to let my aunt know. I've called her a few times already, but she hasn't answered. She's on vacation in Vegas with my mom, so they're probably still sleeping. And Dre's father is deceased."

"Okay. Sorry for your loss," the officer replies.

"Thanks. Dre was like a brother to me. We all grew up together," Dionna responds. "I'll be sure to have my aunt contact you."

"Ray, one more thing," the officer says.

"Yes sir," I speak respectfully.

He voices sternly, "The next time you see someone outside the house, don't go chasing them. We appreciate you giving us a description of the person, but leave all of the chasing suspects to us. You could have been killed."

"Yeah, you're right! I thought about that after the fact. It was kinda stupid to go outside instead of just hiding in the house," I divulge.

"No, Ray. It wasn't kinda stupid, it was very stupid. That guy could've shot you if you would've caught up to him," Dionna chimes in a loud tone.

I realize that now is the time to grab my opportunity by the horns and ride that mother fucker. If I insert the new information now, it'll seem like it's natural as hell. The cops will be intrigued by what I'm going to tell them. I hope

Dionna doesn't mind, but at the end of the day, it doesn't really matter. The name of the game is cover and concealment.

"Oh shit!" I say loudly as I act like an idea just came to me.

"What's wrong Ray?" the officer inquires.

"Well, you said all information could be useful. And when Dionna said I could've gotten shot, it made me think about what happened last night," I answer.

"Damn, Babe, I didn't even think about last night. My mind is so blown right now," Dionna phrases.

"What about last night?" asks the officer.

"I ain't trying to be no snitch, so I don't know if I should even be mentioning it," I state.

"This isn't the streets. I'm not gonna label you a snitch. My job is to solve this case. Now, if something from last night can be helpful, I suggest you or Dionna let it be known," the cop urges.

"Well, last night around ten, me, my niece, and Dionna were at St. Marks Park in Linden when a car pulled up and shot at us. We all ducked down to dodge the bullets and eventually the car sped off" I narrate.

"Really? Did you file a police report?

Dionna answers, "No, we didn't. I was so shaken up that I just wanted to get away from there. I was terrified out of my mind."

"And nobody was hurt, so we figured that

reporting the shooting would be all one big waste of time," I add. "Plus, talking to the cops ain't all that popular."

"I get it. I really do, but that shooting from last night has to be tied to your cousin's murder. Someone probably had beef with your cousin and wanted to retaliate against him, so they went after you. Unfortunately, they finally caught up to your cousin. We're gonna need you two to come down to the station and answer some more questions. Just give us a second," the cop articulates.

I must be a goddamn genius. I knew the cop would surmise that someone was after Gary and attempted to get back at him by coming after Dionna. He thinks that my niece and I were almost collateral damage. They'll follow that trail for forever and never find a thing. I'm good with that because there's nothing there to find. We walk to Dionna's front door and try to go in the house. A cop stands in front of the door and blocks us from going inside the house. Another officer is heading our way. The officer starts to walk towards the front door of the house. As he's walking towards us, he tells Dionna that nobody can enter the house until the cops finish finding evidence. Dionna's upset that she can't go in the house again, but she understands.

There are many media outlets outside the house reporting on the murder. Also, there are a lot of neighbors outside asking questions about what happened. One of Andre's neighbors yells at Dionna and tells her to come here. Dionna walks off the porch in the direction of her neighbor.

"I know this lady just wants to be nosy," Dionna assures.

"Well, you don't need to talk to her anyway. It's none of her business what happened," I state.

"You know you're one hundred percent right," Dionna says. "I'm not even going over there. I really don't feel like it anyways. I need to sit down."

Dionna and I turn around and walk toward the car, so she can sit down. Dionna doesn't like the fact that all of these strangers are in and out of the house, but it's her cousin's place and she can't go in it. While we're sitting in my car, Dionna's phone rings. It's her mother returning her missed calls with her aunt by her side. She tells her mother about what happened to Dre and she breaks down crying and screaming along with her aunt. Dionna, who had gained her composure, begins crying uncontrollably again. I'm in a world wind of guilt, but I'm also filled with the satisfaction of having settled a score. I've removed a tremendous burden from over my head.

Dionna and I are getting very listless just sitting in the car. We need some movement and something to eat. I tell Dionna that since we're not doing anything, we should go get something to eat. She admits that she's hungry and is down for us to bounce. I start the car and start backing up. I'm maneuvering around all of the cop cars and people walking to and fro. One cop runs over to the window of the car and motions for me to roll it down. I stop the car and roll down the window.

"Officer, I know what you're gonna say, but we've been sitting here for a while and we got hungry, so we just wanna go grab a bite and we'll be right back," I deliver.

He replies, "Oh, I'm not worried about that. However, we do have a potential lead from one of the neighbors I wanted to ask you about quickly."

"Okay, what's the lead?" Dionna asks.

"One of your neighbors said she saw a burgundy Honda Accord parked here around the time of the murder and then it was gone by the time she woke up. We think that could have been the car the killer or killers were driving," he narrates. "I'm hoping you guys could help me with finding that car."

Dionna answers, "I wish I could help, but I can't think of anyone I know with a burgundy Accord. I've never seen one parked out here either."

"Are you sure? You can't think of anyone?"

"No, I'm sorry. I don't have a clue. My cousin didn't have many people around. It just wasn't his thing," Dionna notifies.

The cop looks at me and asks, "What about you? Do you know about the car or whose it may be?"

"Sorry, I wish I could help, but this is my first time here. I don't know have any info about the car," I respond.

The cop states, "Damn, we were hoping that would be the break the case open. Well, go get something to eat and we'll see you soon".

Dionna and I finally weave through the sea of people and cars. We make it to the street and pull off. Dionna is executing a mental raid on herself. She's mumbling softly as she tries to recall if she's ever seen one of Dre's friends in that kind of car. I wish I could turn to her and tell her to stop wracking her brain, but I can't. I know she's never going to remember whose car it is because she's never seen it. The fact is that the car that AK and I drove here was that burgundy Honda Accord. The only time I was ever in that car was when we murked Dre.

They'll never tie that car to me because there is no tie. The only person who knows I was in that car is AK. The fiend who he got the car from doesn't even know I was in the car. All roads of Gary's murder lead far from me and AK and I wouldn't have it any other way. Dionna and I go to a wing spot to grab some much needed grub. We talk and eat. Dionna is still in shock from seeing her cousin's dead body. While we're eating, the cops call Dionna and tell her they want to meet us at the station. Dionna and I finish eating and drive to the station for more questioning.

# CHAPTER 12

I pull up to the crib and go inside. AK is in the living room looking intensely at me when I come through the threshold. He looks at me hoping I'll say something, but I don't. Instead, I walk to my room without making any further eye contact. I go to my room and flop on the bed as if I'm angry or frustrated. AK storms into my room behind me.

AK asks, "You good son?"

"Yeah, yo. I'm good. Couldn't be any better," I answer.

"Nigga you don't seem like it. You come through the door and don't say shit and then you crash land on ya bed like something ain't go right," AK explains sternly.

I inquire, "That's what you came up with? Is something wrong with you?"

AK responds, "Hell yeah, I'm good, but I can

tell you didn't get da glove. You acting all sad and shit and that's not like you. It's all good we'll be aight."

I bury my face in my pillow and start laughing. AK thinks I'm crying in anger from not retrieving the glove used in Gary's murder. He stands over me just looking. I'm laughing profusely and tears are streaming from my eyes because AK thinks I'm crying. Eventually, AK realizes that I'm laughing and not crying and gets mad.

"Yo, you got me thinking that you were fucked up, so I was fucked up. You a piece of shit! I'm over here worried and you over there playing. I should've known better than to fall for that dumb shit. You got me good as hell," AK confesses.

I say while laughing, "I know I got you good as fuck. You don't gotta tell me. You was all concerned. Fuck that. You was shook!"

"I was concerned, but I was never shook nigga. You know we don't do shook. We handle shit," AK assures.

I stand up and try to give him a pound, but he playfully pushes me away. I attempt to give him a handshake and he reluctantly gives me one. I tell him that the glove will never be seen again. He's souped up that I was able to get it off successfully. I tell him that Dionna is really broken up over the murder. He thinks that she'll be fine in time and doesn't make a big deal of it.

"But, I really got something that's gonna fuck ya head up!" I voice.

AK says excitedly, "Nigga, this whole shit is already a movie or some shit. It can't be more yo!"

"My nigga there is more! Peep this shit yo. So Gary isn't Derek. Gary turned out to be Dionna's cousin named Dre. She said they grew up together like siblings," I narrate.

"What the fuck yo. Nigga you playing! Son, you gotta be, AK vocalizes.

"I'm not playing yo! This is real shit I'm spitting to you. I can't make this shit up," I assure.

"All I can say is un-fucking-believable! Movie shit for real for real!" AK screams.

"Yo, I got something else on my mind that I gotta tell you. Shit is serious," I voice.

"I ain't falling for another one of your jokes, so you can chill," AK shoots back.

I speak honestly, "Yo, this whole murder shit got me on some other shit. When we started, I never expected that we'd murk somebody."

"Hell yeah nigga! Me either," AK comments. "Shit got wild, but we did what we had to do."

"Yeah, we did, but damn. I murked my girl's cousin. That shit is too close for comfort. That's not how we move," I convey.

"You right, but shit happens in this life we chose and we got away with da shit, so it is what it is," AK passionately verbalizes.

"It's just that simple for you?" I ask.

"Hell, yeah it is! Shit, you good, I'm good, and the money good. Ain't shit else out here for me really. Sounds like you really got something on your chest," AK articulates.

"Word, but shit ain't that simple to me. It's too hot up here for me. If we had to put in work on Dionna's peeps by coincidence, ain't no telling what other coincidences are lurking that we don't know about," I communicate.

"You really shook over this shit? Where are you going with all this shit you talking about?" AK inquires.

I answer frankly, "Yo, I'm thinking I'm done with the life. No more dice games, no more having mad bitches, and no more drug selling. In fact, I'm done with Jersey period."

"Nigga, what da fuck you talking about?" AK asks.

"Yo, I'm outta here is what I'm saying. I know a spot down south that I can tuck off in and be good. Da bread I got is enough to hold me for a while," I answer.

"Down south? How you gonna move to da south? Do you know what's down there? Ain't it only dirt roads down there?" AK asks.

"Son, it's cool down there. I can get low and focus on my schooling. Shit, we can't hustle forever," I respond.

"Son, and where does that leave me? How I'm gonna eat if you bounce?" AK inquires.

"Yo, you can keep all the product from what we just got from Gary and I'll take half da bread. You'll be good," I explain.

"Seems like you got it all worked out. But, fam, once I get rid of the shit we got off Gary or whatever that nigga name is, that leaves me ass out," AK narrates.

"How you figure that?" I ask.

"Man, you know how I do with my bread. I live! That shit ain't gonna last long without a new connect. Gary gone, so I'll need a new supplier. I ain't gonna have shit soon," AK remarks.

"You'll get on ya feet again. You da best at this street shit, but for me, I gotta go. I'm gonna push up on Dionna and see if she wanna go down south with me," I vocalize.

"Nigga, it's bad dope! Stay up here and help me find a new connect," AK says.

"Fam, I can't. I don't wanna be that guy who stays in the streets too long and it costs me my life or my freedom," I say.

"Yo, we not gonna get caught! We been doing this shit for forever. We too smart for the pigs. They can't see us," AK assures.

"I feel you, but it's over for me. I hope you ain't mad, but we both men and men make hard decisions. You my brother, but I gotta do this for me," I convey.

"True," AK says.

AK walks out of my room and goes to his. I can tell AK is beyond upset, but he'll just have to understand. Men do what's best for themselves and their family. That's all I'm doing. The streets are too hot right now for me to stay up here. I can go down south and get low as hell. I'm tired of the razzle dazzle anyway. It's time to get low and focus on my degree. I see an opportunity for me to better myself, so I gotta take it.

I pick up my phone and call Dionna. She answers the phone and I tell her of my intentions to move down south. She isn't the least bit happy about my thoughts. I tell her that she can move with me, but she's not feeling me on that. She explains to me that her mother needs her to be close after the way her cousin was murdered. It's crazy that the reason I'm leaving, is the reason that's gonna keep Dionna in Jersey. Talk about how the same thing that makes you laugh makes you cry. She is very adamant about staying in town to console her mother.

"Well listen, I'm not gonna leave until the end of the semester, so there's time for you to change ya mind," I tell.

"Baby, I'm not leaving my mom and my aunt. It's just not gonna happen," Dionna voices firmly.

"I hope you change ya mind, but I know I'm moving for sure. It's too crazy and unpredictable up here. The south is calm and chill. That's what I'm looking for," I word.

"So, where does ya move gonna leave us?" Dionna inquires.

"I'm thinking we can do long distance and see how it goes. Maybe you can come visit and you'll like it. At some point, you may want to move down. You never know," I remark.

"I mean, I'll come visit, but I ain't promising nothing. I'm a Jersey girl. I can't see me bouncing," Dionna mentions.

"I'm a Jersey nigga and at one point I couldn't see it either, but now I do. You could be like me one day. I just know that I'm not trying to lose you," I narrate.

"What does ya crazy ass homie think about you moving?" Dionna asks.

"You don't even have to ask. You know he's mad as hell. He told me not to go, but I'm not listening to him. I feel this move in my heart. It gotta be right," I respond.

"You really are feeling this move. That's crazy for real for real," Dionna recognizes.

"I am. I gotta make this move and you'll love it when you come to visit. I promise you Babe," I communicate confidently.

I get off the phone with Dionna and lie on the bed. I think about as many different scenarios as possible on how to make my next move. Fortunately, they all lead to me hopping on a flight and leaving Jersey. The song says, "Real niggas do real things."

# CHAPTER 13

I'm sitting in front of my crib in Columbia, South Carolina. I'm really bugging out over how I made such a drastic move. AK is still mad as hell at me for skating, but he'll be alright. Plus, he swears up and down that I'll be moving back up top before long. Saying Dionna is devastated is an understatement. She was totally against me moving down south. But for me, I'm enjoying my time down here. It's real laid back and precisely what I am looking for. Sirens aren't blaring every ten seconds and I'm not in position to have to shoot somebody or get locked up for pushing weight.

I can't front like the game wasn't fun as hell though. I'd be lying if I said that. The game is something I've known for years now and I'm sure I'll miss it. However, I just have to find something else to occupy my time. School has started back and I'm sure I'll make some new friends. I've always been good at meeting new people, so that's not going to be a problem. I was able to transfer from my job in New Jersey to South Carolina, so I'm all squared away there. I start next week. Hopefully, I like it as much as I did in Jersey.

I know one thing that I'm never going to get used to and that's the heat. It's 101 degrees out here and my neighbor said that this isn't even hot for down here yet. I hit my stash a little bit to furnish my new apartment. I had to do it big for my new crib. Anything less would be beneath me. I'm really gassed up because this spot I got down here would be at least fifteen hundred dollars a month in New Jersey.

I faintly hear my phone ringing. I tap my pocket, but it's not in there. I remember I left it sitting by the door on the charger. I zoom over to the phone and look at the call display screen. It's AK calling me. I answer the phone.

"Yo, what's good nigga?" I ask.

"Ain't shit up here. You know shit been dead since you bounced. It ain't da same no more," AK confesses.

"I feel you, but you gonna be straight. You always straight. Besides, I know you got enough bitches to keep you fully occupied," I orate.

AK shoots back, "Hell yeah! I'm up here eating! I got bitches in the professional world now, but I still need my main man to run with."

I know man. I know, but I ain't coming back. That ain't happening. I'm about to see what and who the south has to offer. I know you feeling me on that," I say.

"Yeah, nigga I'm feeling you. We men and men make men moves. We've always been that way," AK voices.

I respond, "No doubt. I know you doing good up there, so I ain't even gonna ask. The hood loves you nigga!"

"Yeah, I'm good on my health, but I could be doing better on my finances. Prices went up on the keys since Gary ain't around no more you feel me, so I ain't eating like we used to," AK explains.

"Damn, yo! I kinda feel bad about how all that shit went down. I know you taking a crazy hit financially behind that nonsense. Yo, let me know if I can help you in any way. You know I got you," I verbalize sincerely.

"Yo, on some real shit, you can help me," AK utters.

"Yeah? How? What you need?" I inquire.
"My nigga! Yo, I need to hold a few dollars til I get on my feet," AK answers.

"No doubt. How much you thinking?" I inquire.

"Yo, I don't need much. I'm just thinking like twenty-five grand, but I can rock with twenty," AK responds.

"Damn, yo! Twenty-five is steep! I can't do

twenty-five or twenty. Shit, max I can hit you with is five grand," I state.

"Five grand? You can't spare a lil more for ya boy?" AK asks.

I speak, "Nah, that's max yo. I'm paying bills, my tuition, and just living. I got more going out than coming in."

"Oh word. I feel you. Bet, I'll make the five work. And one other thing," AK utters.

I verbalize, "True. Let me know."

"Yo, I need you to link me with some of your peoples down there. I know you met some dudes who got shit for da low," AK states.

I answer, "I know a few white boys from my school down here who are moving heavy weight, but that ain't my lane anymore. I'm clean fam."

"Hold up my nigga. It sounds like you saying you won't link me with your guy down there?" AK shoots.

"Son, he's not really my guy. I know dude from class and we hung out before, but that's it. I don't really fuck with him like that," I remark.

AK asks, "So are you gonna make the link for me or not?"

"You know you're my nigga if you don't get no bigga! Of course I'm gonna make the link," I assure.

"Good looks on that. For real. For real," AK says.

I convey clearly, "Give me a couple of days to link with him and I'll hit you back, but like I said,

I don't know him like that. So, I'm not vouching for him."

"Bet. I feel you on that. I just need the link. Cause these niggas up here buggin on da prices," AK confesses. "I'll take ya five and flip that bitch Olympic gymnast style."

I voice, "Shit, you know everything post nine eleven is high as hell. And I know ya flip game is crazy!"

"AK hell yeah! It's hard to move anything up here. Shit locked down," AK complains.

I reply, "Nigga I'm sure it is! Madmen flying planes into skyscrapers tend to change a lot of shit."

"My nigga, you talking some real shit," AK voices enthusiastically.

I hear a beep from my phone alerting me that someone is calling me. I look at my phone screen and see it's Dionna calling me. I'm delighted to see she's calling.

"Yo, that's ole girl calling me. I'm bout to dip, but I'll hit you with that info in a few days," I speak.

"You a old in-love ass nigga. Tell D I said what up. Holla at ya father figure," AK utters.

I shoot back immediately before I switch calls, "Fuck outta here nigga!"

"D, what's up baby? How you?" I ask.

"Hey, big head. I'm good. How are you?" she asks.

I answer, "I'm glad you're good. I'm good for

the most part."

"Hmm, I don't hear you say for the most part very often. However, every time you say for the most part there is always something bothering you," Dionna comments.

"Oh, you think you know me?" I ask.

"No, I don't think I know you. I know I know you. So, you might as well tell me what's going on," Dionna says.

"Aight, I'll put you on. So basically, AK wants me to grant him a favor that I'm reluctant to grant him," I tell.

"I've never heard you be reluctant to grant AK a favor in my life," Dionna voices. "It must be something morally compromising."

"Nah, it isn't morally compromising. It's really just none my business to be involved in. That's my only reservation," I explain.

"Well, I'm not gonna tell you what to do, but I will tell you to ask yourself if he'd do whatever the favor is for you," Dionna verbalizes.

I reply, "That's an easy answer. I know for a fact that he would do it for me."

"So, I don't see why you are so reluctant. Grant him the favor and get out the way," Dionna states.

"True that! I already told him I would. Thanks for listening D," I remark

"Anytime Babe. Well, I just called to hear your voice. Let me go. I'll talk to you later," Dionna words.

"Aight. I love you," I say.

Dionna utters, "I know you do. I love you too."

I hang up the phone and go open my textbook. I have a paper to write and a test to study for. I know it's going to be a long and late night for me. I decide to write the paper first because it's not very lengthy. It's only three pages and I should be able to knock it out fairly quickly, once I figure out what I'm going to write it on.

# CHAPTER 14

It's been two months since I last talked to my main man AK. In all of my years of knowing him, this is the longest period of time we've not spoken. I really don't know what to think because nobody has seen or heard from him. For all I know, he could be locked up. AK could've been moving some work and got arrested. There's even possibility of him being dead. AK has always been hotheaded and emotional, so him popping off on someone is highly possible. I just don't know what the hell to think. AK has been known to dip off for a few days, but this time is different. AK has never completely disappeared for this length of time. I decided not to worry about it anymore and just pray for the best, but prepare for the worst. I live by the motto *"If it ain't rough, it ain't right!"*

I'll be ready to kick it with AK whenever or if

ever he resurfaces. My number is still the same and I don't have any plans on changing it. We've had good times...no, great times! We've made a lot of money for two young boys from Linden. What's also really bothersome is that Dionna and I haven't really been talking too heavy lately. She's been extremely busy between going to classes and work. Not to mention, she's still mourning the death of Gary. Understandably, Dionna's mom and aunt are taking the death of Gary tremendously hard too. There hasn't been one time that Dionna and I talked on the phone that she didn't mention her cousin in some way, shape, or form. I really don't like hearing her go on and on, but I have no choice. Under normal circumstances I don't mind listening to my girl sob, but now it's different. It's different because every word she utters about her cousin makes me mentally relive the night I killed him.

What bothers me even more about listening to her talk about her cousin is how she revered him. My baby Dionna is severely disillusioned about who her cousin was and the life that he led. Dionna and her mother are under the belief that Gary was an upstanding and law-abiding citizen, but they couldn't be more wrong. That nigga Gary was putting in mad work on the streets. He supplied a lot of New Jersey and Philly with product. He even had a couple bodies on him too. I can't front though; Gary was smooth as hell with his. He was like a well-oiled machine when it came to running his criminal enterprise. What was even doper about how he did his thing is that he worked alone. He didn't have mad boys that were a part of his network. I guess that's how he was able to stay undetected completely by the police and his family.

Dionna, her mom, and aunt thought he took some money he got from a lawsuit and invested it. He had them believe that he was living off of his prosperous investments. Dionna talks about how he had a great job and wore suits to work, but little does she know that it was all a façade. Don't get me wrong, by all accounts he was a great cousin to Dionna and a fantastic son to his mother, but at the end of the day he was a grimy ass nigga. I'm just being honest. Enough about Gary though. I need to see what's really good with Dionna. I'm missing her like crazy. I already don't get to see her and now we're barely talking, so I'm really kinda fucked up behind this. In fact, I'm just gonna catch a flight up to Jerz on Friday to see her. I know she's not expecting me, so when I pop up at her job, she'll be hyped up. Keeping it real, I'll probably be more gassed than her. I love that woman to death.

I need to get off this damn couch and type this report that's due tomorrow morning for my English class. I walk into my second bedroom and sit at my computer desk. I have to write a literary analysis paper on some stuff we were assigned to read. It has to be at least five pages in length. Writing a five-page paper is nothing for me. I've always been good at writing, so I'm not sweating this paper. I know I'm definitely not cooking now because it's kind of late, but I'm starving. I have to eat something soon before I starve to death.

While I'm planning to take a break, my phone rings. I look over at my phone and see Dionna's name flashing on the screen. I pick the phone up and answer it.

"What up Baby," I ask.

Dionna replies, "Hey big head. What's good? What you into?"

"I'm low. At the crib typing this paper up. On my student shit," I answer.

Dionna states, "True. That's good to hear. I love an educated man. I got some info bout AK for you."

"Word. What you heard? Don't tell me you heard some crazy shit," I utter.

"You remember Mia the one from Montclair?" Dionna asks.

I respond as I try to remember, "Nah, I don't know who that is."

"Yes, you do! AK was fuckin wit her. The girl from the fashion show that you stripped at," Dionna explains.

"Oh hell yeah, I do! AK fucked her in the bathroom after the fashion show," I recall.

"Yes! That's the one. Well, I saw her on campus and she said AK got locked up in New

York when they were out there like two months ago," Dionna recites.

"Get the fuck outta here! That's why the nigga been MIA. Damn, that's crazy," I shoot back.

"I know right! Glad, he ain't dead," Dionna vocalizes.

"True, I know she told you what happened," I voice.

"Yeah, she said that AK and some dude was arguing over a parking space and before you know it, AK was stomping dude out. Then the police locked him up," Dionna narrates.

"Damn, that's sounds just like AK. I wonder what jail they took him to," I say.

"She didn't say and I didn't think to ask. I'll see if I can get her number and call her to see if she knows," Dionna declares.

I say, "Aight Babe. Yeah, do that and let me know when you find out something."

Dionna and I get off the phone. I'm relieved to know that AK isn't dead. Also, I'm elated to know that he's not locked up for drug trafficking. He's probably facing an assault charge or something light.

I'm starving and a pizza would be good as hell right now. The only question is if I should go pick it up or have it delivered. Delivery it is. No need to waste time going to pick the pizza up when I can use this time to get some of this paper knocked out. I call the pizzeria and order a pepperoni pizza with extra sauce. As soon as I hang up the phone, I start clicking keys on this keyboard. I have already mentally written the paper, so it's just a matter of putting it on paper. While I'm typing, I hear a knock at my door. I jump up and head over to the window to look out and see who it is. I see the pizza company's placard on top of a car. I leave the window and go over to the door.

"Who is it?" I ask loudly.

"Pizza delivery," a man answers.

I open the door and the pizza delivery man is standing there holding a pizza box. Strangely, he doesn't look as comfortable as he normally does. He looks like something is bothering him. Also, he's staring at me as if he wants to tell me something, but can't. The delivery guy hands me the pizza and I take it.

"You good?" I ask.

"Yeah, I'm fine. Just having a long night. We've been real busy. That's why I'm a little late," he answers.

"Word is bond. Well, hopefully it'll ease up for you," I respond.

"Thanks man. Yeah, I hope so too. The pizza is twelve eighty-seven," the pizza delivery guy says.

I sit the pizza box down on the arm of my couch. I reach in my pocket and pull out a twenty-dollar bill and hand it to him. The guy takes the twenty-dollar bill and starts making change.

"Oh, nah man. You good. I don't need any change," I voice.

"Cool, thanks. I appreciate it," says the delivery man.

I state, "No problem."

I'm closing the door and I hear what sounds like people running. Before I close the door fully, I feel tremendous force pushing on the door. The force on the door is so strong that I'm pushed back and almost fall. However, I keep my balance as I'm realizing what's going on. I'm about to be a victim of a home invasion. I rush toward my bedroom to grab my strap in an attempt to defend myself, but I'm unable to make it there. Two masked gunmen are right behind me and kick me to the floor. They even have the pizza delivery guy in here too. I guess they didn't want him to call the cops when he left.

Shit, I know I'm fucked! They got me helpless than a mother fucker. I can't do shit right now. I just gotta see how this plays out. If I'm lucky, I'll catch these niggas slipping and I'll be able to turn the table on them. I'm beyond livid, but I'm not scared. I can't say the same for the pizza delivery guy. His punk ass is sprawled on the floor beside me boo-hooing. One of the home invaders hits me in the back of the head with the gun. I lose a lot of the fight I had in me after the blow. It definitely calmed me down.

Fortunately, the blow doesn't knock me out, but it does make me focus. I zero in on the black air forces the intruder is wearing. They look like the same sneakers that one of the dudes who lives in the apartment complex had on one day. I see the same yellow paint on the intruder's sneakers as I did on the apartment complex resident's footwear.

"Where's da fucking money nigga?" the gunman with the blue facemask asks angrily.

"Yeah, we know you got it bitch nigga! Give that shit up before shit get real ugly for you," the gunman in the black ski mask says.

"I'm just a school boy. I don't know what the fuck y'all niggas is talking about. I ain't got shit!" I shoot back quickly.

One of the gunmen kicks me in the ribs and then points his gun at the back of my head. The kick in the ribs is so forceful that it knocks the wind out of me. I curl up in pain and I'm certain that my ribs are broken. The gunman cocks the gun to show me that he's not playing any games. The gunman orders the pizza delivery guy to get up. He complies with his order and slowly stands up. He hands the pizza guy some plastic zip ties and motions him over to me. The pizza guy walks over to me and kneels down. The gunman orders me to put my hands behind my back. I place my hands behind my back while I'm lying on the floor in agony.

One gunman says, "Tie this mother fucka up right now!"

The intruder who had the gun to my head

moves out the way. Both gunmen point their guns at us. The pizza guy places the zip ties around my wrists. Next, they order him to lie down beside me. He does as he's ordered and lies down. One of the gunman zip ties his legs and arms. Both gunmen approach me and stand me up. I wince in pain as I'm being stood up. I stand up, but am wilted over. My midsection is killing me. As I look at their stature, I realize that they're the same size as two dudes who live a few doors down from. The two of them are always ice grilling me when I pull up to the crib. Come to think of it, one of these dudes even sounds like the guy who asked me for a loosie one day. I knew they were sizing me up.

"We just here for the money. That's it. We gonna find it one way or the other, so it's in your best interest to just give it up," voices one of the intruders as he stands in my face.

The other one speaks, "If you don't tell us we gonna fuck you up some more and we gonna fuck ya crib up too. We can do this da easy way or da hard way."

I know now that I have a decision to make. I know what they're saying is one hundred percent right. They have all the time in the world to look for the money and my apartment isn't that big, so they'll definitely find it. I'm reluctant to just give up my bread, but they've already shown that they'll use violence and they clearly have the upper hand. The longer they're here increases the chances that something sideways will happen to us. I have to bite the bullet on this one.

"Aight man. Aight. It's in the bedroom," I say reluctantly.

"That's what da fuck I'm talking about! Get ya ass in da bedroom then and get us our fuckin money nigga!" one of them verbalizes.

They nudge me as I walk to my guest bedroom. We go in the room and I pause. I think if there is any way to get away without giving them a dime of my money, but I'm drawing a blank. This is the part of the game that I never wanted to be a victim of, but it comes with the territory. I raise my head and take it on the chin.

I ask, "One of you got a shank or something?"

"What da fuck for?" one of them asks back.

"You gonna need it to get the money that's why," I answer arrogantly.

"Nigga we don't bring knives to gunfights! Hell no, we ain't got no fucking knife," the masked gunman replies with a scoff.

One of the invaders runs out of the room. I hear him rummaging through my kitchen drawers. He promptly returns with two of my kitchen knives.

"Aight, bitch nigga. Show us where it is!" one orders.

"Yeah, and you better not be lying or sending us on a wild goose chase," the other one chimes in.

I say, "It's in the cushion of the futon. You gonna have to cut the futon open to get to it though. Start cutting in the top left corner of the mattress. I promise you it's in there."

"For your sake, it better be," one replies.

The gunman with the blue mask goes over to the futon and starts cutting as directed. Moments later, he cuts the mattress to the point where the money is exposed. He makes a few more cuts on the mattress and then starts grabbing the money. He feverishly starts packing the money in a black duffle bag that he has. Both gunmen are laughing in a sinister fashion as they steal the loot.

One sarcastically voices, "Oh shit! You had some paper! Glad we could get this up off you!"

"Whatever man!" I remark.

"You got more money in here anywhere?" one inquires.

"Yo, it don't matter. We gotta go. We got more than what we thought we were gonna get, so we gotta bounce. Plus, somebody gonna be looking for the pizza delivery nigga anyway," one voices.

"Oh shit! I forgot about that that dude. I should go slap his ass for being a pizza delivery guy," he shoots back as he laughs.

The other gunman looks at me and says, "Aight, get ya ass down on the floor again nigga! We gotta tie ya feet up, so you won't be able to call the cops as soon as we leave.

I'm more than happy to comply because that

means they're not going to kill us. I get down on the floor and they zip tie my legs together. They close the room door behind them as they leave. I yell out to the pizza man and he yells back. He's in good shape and hasn't been harmed. I manage to get to my feet and make it into the living room. The pizza guy is on the floor. I don't see my cell phone anywhere and the delivery guy doesn't have one. I go in my room and call 9-1-1 from the landline.

# CHAPTER 15

It's been three months since I got robbed at my apartment. If I said getting held at gunpoint hasn't changed me, I'd be lying. I'm definitely not the same anymore. One way I've changed is that I'm always on high alert. I don't trust anyone if I don't already know them. Additionally, I notice that I'm extremely cautious of my surroundings. Now, when I go into a restaurant, I look for an additional exit just in case I have to get out of dodge quickly. I can't waste valuable time trying to find an exit if something horrific goes down. Those few extra seconds of indecision could be the difference between life and death.

I know one big difference in me is that I'm paranoid now. Fortunately, it's not a debilitating paranoia. I just know that I'm not as protected as I once thought I was. The first couple of days after the home invasion I wouldn't put my gun down. It was so bad that I slept with it on my chest. I never put the strap down inside the house. If I went to the bathroom, I'd take it in there with me. When I go out and see people who have the same body statures and complexions of the two fellas that robbed me, I can't help but wonder if they're the guys who got me. Magically, my old neighbors moved away.

Understandably, I've been upset about the home invasion and robbery that occurred. Shoot, anybody would. I was tremendously mad at the two dudes who ran up in my spot. They robbed me for one hundred thousand dollars and there's no way I'm getting that back from them. Losing a hundred thousand dollars in seemingly the blink of an eye was a crazy loss for me. That was my nest egg for if times got tough, but now it's gone. The crazy thing is that the money isn't the biggest loss of the situation. Those men stole my sense of security that I doubt I'll ever get back. They really caught me slipping and I'm more vexed at myself for that than I am mad at the two intruders.

However, I've have been feeling more secure at home. I knew I'd never sleep another comfortable night in the apartment I got robbed in, so I moved. My new place is in a gated community with a security guard at the gate. An unknown person can't just access the grounds to the complex. Another layer of security to my new place is that guests have to be buzzed into the condo building. The only other option to gain access to the building is to have tenant credentials to open the access door.

My new spot is posh. I have stainless steel appliances and granite countertops in the kitchen and bathroom. This place has hardwood floors in all of the rooms except for the bathroom and kitchen. The floors in the bathroom and kitchen are marble. I can honestly say that I'm living pretty damn good. I'm kicking myself because I should've been living here from jump street. If I lived here from day one of dwelling in the south, I would've never gotten robbed. Having a place that's safe and adorned with modern amenities is not cheap. This place is expensive like a condo in Jersey City.

My precious bank account that was once filled with a lot of zeros is now not so hefty. It was once an obese man and now it's dwindled down to a guy who needs to gain a few pounds. At this point, there's no going back to a cheaper place because my peace of mind means everything. Also, there's no chance that I'm going to let my account get much lower than it already is. It's just not my style. Living a life of subsistence has never been for me and it won't ever be. For the first time in years, I don't have any money stashed at the crib. My job is only part-time, so that's not paying me anything that I can really put up. That money is to keep Uncle Sam happy and to have some light change in my pocket.

I decided that I have to get my change back up. I'm not playing any games out here in these streets. I just landed at Newark Airport. I felt it was time for a visit, so I grabbed a flight up. My brother is picking me up. He's the only one who knows that I'm in town. You can't let everyone know your moves. Besides, popping up in the hood is fun. It seems like people are more excited to see you when they don't expect you to be around. I see my brother approaching in his car. I wave my hand and walk toward the curb. My brother pulls up and pops the trunk. I throw my bag in the trunk and get in the car.

"What's good nigga?" I ask as we dap each other up.

He answers, "Ain't shit. Trying to see what's good with you."

"Word. I'm chilling. I'm trying to see what's good with you," I reply.

My brother answers, "Same shit, different toilet. You know I'm fucking with these bitches heavy!"

"Well, I'm glad to see that everything is normal then. Know them hoes love you," I shoot back as I chuckle.

"That's always! That shit ain't never gonna change," he says.

I voice, "Nigga never…ain't no need for it to change."

"Nope. Speaking of…I'm surprised you didn't

get Dionna to come scoop you," my brother mentions.

"You know that's my normal, but she been kinda hit or miss lately, so I'm just gonna pop up on her at work or some shit," I state.

"No doubt. I knew it had to be something going on if ole girl ain't scoop you up. No fronting, I'm glad she didn't come get ya bitch ass," he speaks.

"Yeah? Why you say that?" I inquire enthusiastically.

He remarks sarcastically, "Cause if she would've came and got you, I wouldn't have seen your duck ass the entire time you were here."

"Fuck you nigga! You bugging," I say as I crack up laughing.

I'm mad close with my brother. We've always been mad tight. A breath of air can't get between us. We are waiting on our other brother to hit the streets, but he doing a bid right now. It's all good because his time will be up in a little bit. As we drive, we plan on hitting Northern State to visit him. It'll be dope to pop up on him when he's not expecting it. I ask my brother if he's seen AK. He told me he's seen him at a bar in our neighborhood almost every day because he's dating a chick who works there.

"Son, around what time do he be in there?" I ask.

"Shit, normally around now. It's been like clockwork lately," my brother tells me.

I state, "Yeah, that's AK's normal. He def not fucking her yet because he wouldn't be in her face like that if he was. Take me over there, yo."

"Aight, I need a drink or two anyway," my brother shares.

Ten minutes later we pull up to the bar. We walk inside and sit at the bar. I do a quick visual scan, but I don't see AK anywhere. I was really hoping he'd be in here. I really need to see that nigga. It's urgent me and him speak. My brother informs me that the lady working the bar is the one AK is kicking it with. I'm glad she's in here because according to my brother that means he'll be in here. The bad part is that if he doesn't show up here, I won't know where to find him. The bartender walks over to us and places some napkins in front of us.

"Hey, Kev," she says.

"What up? How you?" my brother Kev asks.

She answers, "I'm good. Can't complain…besides nobody wants to hear it anyway."

"I feel you. Ain't gonna change nothing," Kev remarks.

"Right, you drinking ya normal today?" she asks.

"Yeah, and let me get some wings too," Kev answers.

The bartender looks over at me and asks, "What can I get for you today?"

"I'm good with a Sprite, but don't put a lot of

ice in it. Let me get some wings too with blue cheese," I answer.

"Okay, it'll be out soon," she says as she giggles.

I comment, "Let me in on da joke. I wanna know what's funny."

"It ain't nothing serious, but y'all sound just alike. It's almost da same voice," the bartender comments.

Kev says, "This my damn brother that's why."

"Now it makes sense. I ain't even know you had a brother. He don't ever be here," the bartender speaks.

"He live down south now, but he just moved down there," Kev replies.

"Yeah, yo. I'm born and raised right here in Linden. I'm Ray," I chime in.

"That's what's up! I'm Kelly. Yo, it's crazy how much y'all sound alike. Shit, even kinda look alike," Kelly states.

"Cut it da fuck out Kelly. Here you go with that bull shit," Kev voices while laughing.

"Whatever Kev! You know you heard that shit before," Kelly words assuredly.

More customers walk in and Kelly walks away from us to serve them. My brother and I both look at Kelly's ass when she walks away. My brother looks at me and smirks. Kelly has a fat ass to say the least. She's also very attractive. I'm not surprised one bit that AK is making her acquaintance. She is his speed hands down. I've never seen AK with a busted chick in my life. As we sit here, more people from Linden come in the bar. Several people I haven't seen in years are in here.

"Oh shit, Ray! What da fuck nigga," Jay, who is one of my former classmates, yells when he notices me.

"My nigga!" I exclaim when I see him.

"How you?" Jay asks.

"My nigga, I'm great! Everything good!" I reply.

Jay, my brother, and I sit at the bar and converse. My brother buys him a shot and then Jay buys him one in return. Kelly hangs with us every chance she gets. She has mad jokes and is real bubbly, so I'm sure her and AK get along perfectly.

Jay says, "I know AK is on his way cause y'all niggas was always together. Y'all mother fuckas was inseparable."

Before I answer, Kelly blurts out, "Wait Ray, I know you not da same Ray that AK is always telling me stories about."

"AK is my nigga! That's my man one hundred grand," I reply sternly.

"Oh, my bad. I didn't even make the down south connection with your name. I had a brain freeze. I heard a lot about you," Kelly articulates.

"It's all good. Dude is like my brother," I utter.

"Well, I guess I ain't gotta tell you that he's on

his way here. Should be walking in at any moment now," Kelly tells.

Kelly leaves to serve other customers. Jay walks away to go shoot pool with my brother. I'm sitting here eating when I feel a poke in my side. I don't have to turn around to know that it's AK. He's the only person who ever would poke me in the side when I wasn't looking. I look over my shoulder and see AK standing there grinning. I stand to my feet immediately. I'm extremely happy to see my boy.

"What's good Ray? Where da fuck you been?" AK asks as we dap each other up.

"Nigga, you know where I been. Shit, where da fuck you been?" I ask sternly.

"Man, I was on some dumb shit. Nigga temper got da best of me. I broke my phone during a situation I had in NY. Told myself I wasn't fucking myself ova no more," AK explains.

"Son, I heard months later about ya situation, but had no clue how to contact you or what spot you were at. And I called everywhere. Had my lawyer friend even try to find you, but she couldn't," I tell.

"Nigga, it's all good. Don't even stress about that jail shit. They dropped the charges anyway. I was really in there just resting. That shit was all my bad over a parking spot," AK narrates.

"No doubt. That's what it is. Shit, you still should've got at my brother when you got out.

You know he has my math," I vocalize.

AK explains himself by saying, "Word, that was my thought. I saw ya brother in passing a few times, but wasn't in position to holla at him. When I finally started seeing him in here, too much time had passed. I wasn't trying to get ya digits from him after so much time had passed. I figured I spit at you whenever we bumped into each other."

"No doubt. Well, I'm here and we're talking, so I guess it went the way you wanted it to," I voice.

"Word. You ain't never lied. You still fresh as hell my nigga! I see the south is treating you good as hell. You living good! I'm glad to see it," AK compliments.

"Yeah, my nigga. I'm living good, but I see you've been living damn good yourself. That's at least a ten-thousand-dollar chain you're wearing. Louie loafers and Gucci shades," I articulate.

AK verbalizes, "Yeah, I been doin my thing lately, but I'm about to be fucked up soon. I see it coming."

"Yeah? You fucked up? How?" I ask in a shocked tone.

"Yeah, yo. I say that because this Dominican nigga I was getting my shit from got bodied out in Newark a few weeks ago. These other niggas out here talking about they dry and ain't shit around," AK summarizes as he sips his drink.

"Damn, yo. My brother told me about some

Dominican nigga dat got bodied in Newark on Summer Ave," I comment.

"Yeah, that was my man, Abraham. He was a real nigga. Was getting me mad birds for da low. Now he gone and the streets dry as hell!" AK states.

I shoot back, "I feel you. I'm fucked up too, well soon anyway. On some crazy shit, niggas ran up in my spot and robbed me for a hundred large. Dat was damn near all my dough. Only bread I got now is what's in da bank and it ain't gonna hold me."

AK yells wildly, "Get da fuck outta here! That's wild as hell! Son, I know that hunnet grand hurt to lose, but at least you here to tell me who did that shit. I'll slide back south with you and body bag them niggas!"

"That's real shit! Losing that bread hurt like a muhfucker, but I left with my life and that is good enough. I guess that was my karma for all da shit I did. I'm off my feet, but I'm still alive," I say.

"I hear you with all that karma shit, but point them niggas out to me though. Anybody who brings harm to you, gotta answer to me and my AK 47," AK remarks.

I convey, "I know it was some niggas that live in the apartment complex I moved out of, but I'm let that shit slide and take it as my karma."

"We know karma comes back to us and I feel that, but them niggas need me to bring them their karma," AK utters.

"Nah fam. That revenge shit is dead! I'm broke and need to get my paper up. That's all I'm looking for," I voice sincerely.

"Aight, if you wanna let that slide. I guess that's what it is. I got a couple dollars, but I don't got no way to flip it. I don't want to wait until I'm on my last dollar and then have to starve. I wanna keep this shit rollin. I know you feel me," AK tells.

I reply, "You know I feel you. My nigga, that's why I'm here. I got this Mexican dude down south that's moving mad work. He ready to hit me off whenever. I'm ready now. I hope you ready."

"You already know I'm ready nigga. This what da fuck I do! I live for this getting money shit. I ain't trying to live no other way," AK boasts.

"That's what da fuck I'm talking about! We bout to get this money again. It's gonna be like old times…if not, better than old times. Da only question, the amount of dough you got to start with," I convey.

AK inquires, "Shit, my nigga. How much bread you thinking we gonna need to get this shit on and popping?"

I respond, "Yo, I'm really thinking no less than twenty-five grand to step to the Mexican dude with."

"Son, that is not the number I had in my fuckin head!" AK shoots back. "I can't do twenty-five!"

"Damn, how much you thinking?" I ask urgently.

AK answers, "I'm thinking ten yo?"

"Damn, only ten?" I inquire.

"Yeah, ten and I can barely do the ten. I'm gonna need to hold a couple of dollars, so I can still live until we start getting the money off da shit," AK expresses.

"My nigga! Least you got ten. My money is fucked up. I don't got shit to go in with, but I'll pay you back ya cut when we get this shit going. And that'll be soon," I voice.

AK speaks, "Hold up my nigga. You my brother! You don't gotta pay me back shit! Ya money is my money."

I cut AK off and say, "My bad bro. I just don't ever wanna come off like I'm trying to exploit our brotherhood. No offense intended."

"Aight! No doubt! None taken. Now, tell me what this Mexican nigga talking about and how you see this shit goin, so we can get this money," AK utters.

Several people sit around us at the bar. I don't know who may be able to hear what I'm about to tell him, so we move to a booth over in the corner of the bar. I tell AK all of the particulars about how I intend to move the product to New Jersey. I also tell AK how much the Mexican dude wants for each kilo we purchase from him. AK is fully on board with everything I'm telling him. AK and I are going to link up with the Mexican tomorrow so we can get the product. We're both excited about the future possibilities.

AK goes back over to the bar to talk to Kelly. I walk over to my brother and dap him up because I'm leaving. I'm borrowing his car, so I can shoot up to Montclair State's campus to see Dionna. I'm sure she's working the counter. I'm just going to pop up and surprise her. I get his keys and exit the bar. I decide to take the scenic route to campus instead of jumping on the Parkway. I haven't been up here in a while, so it'll be good to just cruise through my old stomping grounds.

About a half hour later, I make it to Montclair's campus. I spray some cologne and look myself over. I haven't seen Dionna in a long time, so I have to be fresh and smelling good. I jump out the whip and walk over to the building she works in. As I'm walking along the outside of the building she works in, I look inside. I spot her sitting at the desk. I'm gassed up that she's here. I can't front like she's not looking good as hell. I don't know why I'm acting like I'm surprised because she always looks good as hell. I walk inside and go over to her counter. As I'm approaching the counter, she looks over at me and gives me a warm smile. I smile right back at her.

"What's up stranger? How are you?" I ask.

"I'm good, but if anyone is the stranger it's

you! Thank you very much!" Dionna cracks back.

"Word, I see how you doing it. I'll take that. It's good seeing you… give ya boy a hug or something," I say.

"Don't come in here tryin to order me around. You know I don't play like that," Dionna states sternly.

"Yo, D. It's me…Ray," I comment.

Dionna laughs and states, "Don't be so serious…I was just playing with you. I got ya behind good. That's what you get for not comin up here to see me in so long. But listen, I get off in ten minutes. Wait for me outside and you'll get ya hug then."

"Oh, you funny as hell! You got that off! I'll see you in a minute," I say as I walk outside.

A few minutes later, Dionna walks out and gives me a long hug. Man, I need this right now. Her body is so soft and she smells heavenly. I'm glad she's just as excited to see me as I am to see her. We walk over to her car and post up outside.

"So, what's good?" Dionna asks.

I answer, "Being here with you right now is what's good."

"I'd have to say that's great! I missed you Baby. No, like I really, really missed you," Dionna assures.

"Shit, I missed da hell outta you too," I word sincerely.

"You better had, big head," Dionna tells.

I pull her close to me and say seductively, "I bet you wanna feel my big head in you. I know you do."

"Hmm, maybe if you grow one first," Dionna states jokingly.

We both laugh, as I pretend to beat her up for her joke. As we're play fighting, I catch a glance of a man's fitted cap in her car. I'm slightly taken aback by the hat. Truthfully, I shouldn't be, but I am. I have to ask her about it.

"Is that some nigga's hat in ya back seat?" I ask in a forceful tone.

"Yeah, it is. That was one of my brother's hats. Member I told you about the step show I was in. That's da hat I wore. We all wore hats. You would've known that if you were up here," Dionna articulates.

"Oh shit. That's my bad. You right and I'm tripping. Haven't seen you in a minute, so I was just a little jealous," I convey.

Dionna speaks, "Don't be jealous, but I'll be honest with you. I do be chilling with dudes up here. I don't just sit home and wait for you to call."

I don't really like the news that Dionna just gave me, but there's nothing I can do about it. I'd be a fool to think that she's not hanging with anybody up here. I decide it's better to just bite my tongue and live in the moment. I'll enjoy time with Dionna and not have any drama between us. Dionna follows me back to Linden, so I can give my brother his car back. I walk in the bar and give my brother his keys back. I immediately walk out of the bar and jump in the car with Dionna. We leave there and head to the hotel.

# CHAPTER 16

It's been two months since AK and I met at the bar and agreed to go back into business with each other again. Our brotherhood picked up right where we left off. We are just as tight as we were before the hiatus. We're back to talking every day like we used to. The distance between us has changed the way we interact with one another, but isn't vast enough to decimate our friendship.

AK and I are getting money like never before. He's holding down his part of our new drug enterprise handsomely. The best part about this go round of our operation is that I don't have to drive with any product. My chances of taking a fall for our illegal activities are virtually nothing. I really think I've outdone myself with the scheme that I've engineered to move the product. There are a lot of moving parts involved with the network and it takes a well-prepared mind to make it all work.

I'm at the center of the operation. It all starts with me and that's the way I like it to be. Phase one of my drug enterprise starts with me dropping the money off with my Mexican connect. I love the way he operates. This is all business for the both of us and we treat it as such. He's part of a Mexican cartel, so he can't have any slipups. I'm not trying to see the inside of any prisons or an early death, so I can't have any impediments either.

The money drop is crucial to getting things started off on the right track. Obviously, if the money isn't right, business will be hindered. If business is slowed down, so are profits. We're not having any of that. I don't drop the money to him hand to hand. Instead, I put the money in the trunk of a car and then tell him the location of the car. Next, he has one of his runners go to the car to get the money. After he verifies the bread is in the car, his runner leaves the product.

The next step is where it gets intricate. Instead of going to get the car myself or removing the product myself, I have a flunky pick the car up. He doesn't even know that drugs are loaded into the car. He just thinks that I flip cars. It'll be his word against mine if something goes awry. Then he takes the car to a transport vehicle to be transported up north. The truck service guarantees delivery by an exact date. I use the same person to ship the car up north each time and he ships it in his name. I have to pay him, but that's okay because I just consider it a business expense.

The only drawback about the methods I use is that it's very time consuming. The planning on the front end takes some time, but it's pretty streamlined. Unfortunately, the transporting of the car to New Jersey is the most time-consuming part for me. Unbeknownst to anyone, I actually follow the truck with the car on it all the way to New Jersey. The drive is not extremely long and can be driven in about twelve hours, but truck drivers have a lot of different driving regulations they have to adhere to and that's what makes it time consuming. By law, they can only drive a certain number of hours a day, so I'm often on the road following the truck. Many people would consider what I do to be over the top, but I don't. My main goal is to not get caught and I'm willing to do anything to make sure I don't. I'd rather spend the time on the front end to ensure my load makes it instead of getting jammed by the police. I'd be in jail kicking myself because I was lazy in my illegal enterprise.

However, I don't only follow the truck for me. I also keep a tight eye on it for AK. He's on the receiving end of the car with the drugs in it, so I don't want him to go to pick the car up and two seconds later the police run down on him. I owe it to him to ensure that doesn't happen. Shit, he's the reason why I'm back on my feet. He put all the bread up for us to start getting money again. We've been boys for too long for me not to protect him and the product. I don't want any extra credit for going the extra mile to protect him and the drugs, so I haven't even told him that I follow the load. It's just how we move. We never keep a scorecard of what we do for each other.

I'm out here now floating up the New Jersey Turnpike. We're getting off the Turnpike now in Elizabeth. The car transport driver picked the car up yesterday around 8am and said he'll have the car in Jersey by 4pm today. He's right on time. I got lucky this time because the car I had sent was his last pickup and all of his cars are being delivered in New Jersey. The last time I shipped a car, I was on the road for three days following the car transport driver. The car is being delivered to a mechanic in Elizabeth that AK had arranged. We'll be there in about ten minutes. I decide to call AK to see where he is. The phone rings several times and the finally he picks up.

"Yo! Yo! Yo!" I say repeatedly.

There's a pause and then AK says, "My bad. I had dropped my phone on the damn floor."

"No doubt. No doubt. The truck driver supposed to be there by 4. He didn't say he was gonna be late," I utter.

AK pauses again and voices, "Cool. I'm out here now. Pulled up about fifteen minutes ago. Just sitting here chilling and waiting now."

"That's good shit! Word. Handle ya handle and let me know when you get da shit straight," I verbalize.

"I got you my nigga. I got you," AK assures.

AK hangs the phone up and so do I. I'll be at the location in a few minutes and will be able to rest my brain once the drop is made. A sense of relief always comes over me once everything is settled. It seems like we're getting caught at every light and the lights are taking ten minutes apiece to change. After what seems like another hour, the truck turns on the block that the car is being delivered to. I stop at the corner and park my car. I'm in position to see everything that's going on.

The truck driver stops his truck in the street and goes in the mechanic spot. He has some conversation with a guy who appears to work there. Why isn't AK getting out the car? He normally would've approached the truck by now. Shit, maybe he knows something that I don't. I hope ain't no funny shit go down. As I focus on AK in the car, I notice he's not alone. What the fuck is going on? What is that nigga stalling for? It makes sense that he's not alone because he'll need someone to drive his whip after he picks up the car with the drugs in it.

I want to get out of the car to get a closer look, but I can't risk being seen, so I just chill in the car and watch closely. The truck driver is dropping the car in the parking lot of the mechanic.

Moments later, the car is dropped and the driver pulls off. AK finally gets out of the car and goes to the mechanic spot. I guess he wanted to wait until the driver pulled off or he was finishing getting his conversation with the girl in the car with him. I'll wait for him to pull off before I bounce. Seconds later, the passenger door of AK's car opens. A girl jumps out and goes to the driver's side of his whip.

Damn, she got a dope ass body! I see AK got him another bad bitch. He knows he can pull them. She built just like Dionna! Hold the fuck up...that is Dionna! Why would this nigga have Dionna with him? I can't believe this shit! I know that nigga ain't fucking her! Yo, that bitch is a fucking hoe and I was trying to wife her. Meanwhile, I'm thinking AK got my back and the whole time, he's double dealing like a mutha-fucka. This shit foul as hell!

Hmm, what the fuck should I do? I think I'm just gonna run down on them and let them know that I know what it is. Fuck it! I open the door and jump out the car, but before I close the door I immediately sit back down. This won't end well at all. I'm emotional and there are drugs in the vicinity. If I spaz out, the police will be called and we'll all possibly end up in jail. I got to play this shit just right. Man up nigga! Man up! I pull away from the scene and call Dionna.

She answers, "Hey, Babe!"

I bite my tongue and respond normally,

"What's good Baby?"

"Everything! What you doing?" Dionna asks.

"I ain't doing shit, but I hope to be soon," I shoot back.

Dionna asks, "Oh, is that a fact? What you getting into?"

"Yes, that's an incontrovertible fact. If I'm lucky, it'll be you," I remark.

"Hell yeah, that would be nice, but you kinda far away for that," Dionna states.

"Umm, not quite. I'll be in Linden in a couple of hours," I convey.

Dionna pauses and responds, "Oh! That's what's up Babe! So, you will be definitely getting into me!"

"Yeah, damn right I will! So, I'll be seeing you in a little bit," I say.

"That's cool, but I got some running around to do and then I'll be free. It'll be a few hours before I get free though," Dionna explains.

I reply, "Aight, cool. Well, I'll be around soon, so just call me when you get free. Can't wait to see you!"

"Ok, Ray. Can't wait to see or feel you either! See you in a while, but let me jump off," Dionna articulates.

I hang up the phone without letting my emotions show. It was hard to do, but I can't let her know that I know their secret. I have to put something together to get ahead of this. Should I approach AK individually? Maybe I should just break ties with Dionna and AK and take this one on the chin. Fuck that! I need answers. I know an explanation doesn't change anything, but I need to know if they're fucking each other. Something grimy has to be going on for Dionna not to tell me that she was with AK.

I'm going to follow Dionna because I need to see where she's going. She's probably going somewhere with AK to drop the drugs off and then fuck him. Dionna pulls out of the parking space and into traffic. This is some wild shit to say the least. I can't believe that I'm actually saying that AK and Dionna are creeping behind my back. I call AK back to see what he says about the load of drugs. The phone is ringing.

"Yo, what's up? How you making out with that?" I ask as he answers the phone.

"Damn yo, you beasting! We good! Real good! Calm down nigga. You all thirsty," AK comments.

I reply, "Whateva man. I'm just checking on da shit. Making sure you were good. You know I always be paranoid on delivery days."

"Well, you can relax my nigga. I got da shit and I'm headed to the stash spot now. We smoove as hell like normal. Dig though, let me hit you back cause I ain't trying to drive and talk on the phone with da shit in da car. You know the Dees be lurkin," AK remarks.

"No doubt. Holla at ya boy," I say.

We end the call and I continue following

Dionna. She is driving down North Broad Street towards Newark. I'm several cars behind her just so I won't be detected by her. I really don't have anything to worry about because she normally doesn't pay attention to anything that's not in front of her. A helicopter could fly behind her for an hour straight and she'd never know. We stop at a light and I look in my rearview mirror. To my surprise, I see AK a few cars behind me.

"Fuck!" I yell out.

I hope this nigga didn't see me. It's highly likely he did see me because AK doesn't normally miss a beat. That mother fucker sees everything moving. On the flip side, he wouldn't really be looking for me. Shit, it's only a matter of time before Dionna calls him and tells him that I'll be around. The light changes and the traffic flows again. I'm now watching Dionna and AK simultaneously. I really hadn't planned for this. I have to do something to let AK pass me without making it too obvious. I know what I can do.

While I'm driving, I put my blinker on and get in the turning lane. That will allow AK to drive past me without arising suspicion. To my delight, my move works flawlessly. AK drives past and doesn't even notice me. I let a couple of cars go past and then I get out of the turning lane. I get back in the lane that I was initially in. Gladly, I still have a line of sight on AK, but I've lost Dionna. It's all good because they were heading in the same direction and are most likely going to the same destination.

We cross over into Newark. We're driving past Weequaic Park and AK turns on Lyons Ave. I follow him, but not too closely. Moments later, AK parks the car in front of a crib on Renner Ave. He exits the car and reaches into the trunk. I see him grabbing the bag that has the drugs in it. He walks toward an apartment. I pull into a parking space down the street. Seconds later, Dionna exits the car she was in and they walk in the house together.

I walk up the block and go around the side of the crib. I don't know what apartment they're in, so I'll just see what I can see. As I'm walking around the back of the house, I see a window slightly ajar. I stand below the window and I hear AK's voice faintly from another room. Dionna and AK are having a conversation about me, but I can't quite hear what they're saying. I have to hear what the fuck they're saying.

I have to get inside the apartment. I pull a garbage can over to the window and stand on top of it. I stealthily open the window up and climb inside. I'm in the back bedroom and can hear their conversation without impediment. Dionna is telling AK that I mentioned that I'll be in New Jersey shortly and that she's supposed to be getting up with me.

"Ray is always popping up! You never know when he's gonna pop up. Dude will just be at the park outta thin air," AK reports.

"I know he pops up a lot, but this time it's different. He seemed like he had an agenda," Dionna says in a concerned tone.

AK voices, "Shorty, relax. You all paranoid and shit. That nigga is always like a little bitch when we got a load being delivered."

"I hope you're right, cause it seemed like he knew something. You know he smart as hell and be knowing mad shit. He just be putting shit together," Dionna verbalizes.

AK announces loudly, "Yo, cut that paranoid shit out! If he be putting so much shit together like you saying, then he'd know that I'm fucking you and that we set him up to get robbed. By the way, that was a good ass idea you came up with to rob him."

In the blink of an eye, I've been overtaken with fury. I've never felt rage like this ever in my life. My main man is fucking the lady I love and they set me up to be robbed. Now it all makes sense. That's why he was so quick to give me the bread to give to the Mexican cartel nigga. It was my damn money to begin with. Wow! What pieces of shit they are! I guess he was telling the truth when he told me that my money was his money. Fucking bastards!

Dionna laughs and says, "Well, you right about that. Maybe he ain't as smart as I'm giving him credit for. And of course it was good as hell."

"I know I'm right. Peep this, his dumb ass even believed I got locked up in NY, but didn't contact anyone. And a lawyer he hired couldn't find me in the system," AK voices.

"Yeah, he really is dumb as fuck," Dionna declares.

"Exactly, now since you said fuck. Come over here and let me fuck ya face some more like I was doing when we was by the mechanic spot. This time I'm gonna finish what I started," AK states.

"You so nasty and I fuckin love it!" Dionna asserts.

So, she was giving him head in the front seat. That's what took him so long to get out the fucking car. AK is moaning profusely as Dionna serves him. With each moan, I become angrier and angrier. I'm about to lose my fucking marbles. I hear Dionna choking and gagging while she's sucking AK's dick.

"Just like that! Hell yeah! Yo, ya head game is crazy! I'm gonna buss in ya mouth like how you like it!" AK voices.

I can't take any more of this shit! These mother fuckers are trying to play me the fuck out. They think this shit is a joke. They are in there laughing at me like I ain't that nigga. I start walking toward the window, so I can make my exit. I've heard enough and have the information that I need. I just can't fuck with them anymore. It's a damn wrap for them.

"Make sure you kiss him later, so he can taste my babies," AK jokes sinisterly.

Dionna stops giving him head and states while

chuckling, "Oh my fuckin gosh, you are so gangster. I love when you talk that slick shit."

It's clear that they got me twisted like Keith Sweat. Fueled by rage, I turn away from the window. Next, I creep into the hallway and stop by the door of the room that AK and Dionna are in. I stealthily peek in the room. Fortunately, AK's gun is sitting on the chair by the door. AK's back is to me and his pants are down around his ankles. Dionna is on her knees still sucking AK off. I run in the room and grab his gun immediately. Taken by surprise, AK jumps back and stumbles as he pulls his pants up. Dionna gets off of her knees and stands up.

"Oh my goodness! Ray, let me clear all this up!" Dionna voices loudly.

"Fuck both of y'all! Ain't no explaining. I guess you gonna explain to me how you was sucking this bitch ass nigga's dick!" I voice sternly.

"I don't care about that gun. You ain't gonna do shit with it, so stop waving that shit around like you tough," AK voices confidently.

Dionna cries and apologizes while I hold them at gun point. AK is acting very casual about the situation and is rocking back and forth as he laughs at me. I order him to stop moving, but he's hardheaded as normal. Next, AK makes a move to rush me, but I saw it coming, so I shoot him several times. He falls to the floor dead. Dionna screams out and runs to him while he's on the floor.

"That's how you feel about that nigga?" I ask angrily.

Dionna replies while sobbing, "Damn right! He was there for me when you abandoned me. You left me here by myself after my cousin died. AK consoled me and helped me get through a tough time."

"It was a bad time for me too. You could've moved when I moved, but you chose not to," I shoot back in my defense.

"I thought about it after a while, but when AK told me that you're the one who killed my cousin, I could never move with you like that," Dionna comments.

I say in a shocked tone, "I had no idea you knew about that. It wasn't meant to go down like that," Dionna explains.

"I know. AK explained it all to me. I know it was just part of the game. Shit happens, so don't judge me for doing what I did with AK. I needed someone and he was that someone."

"I feel you, but I can't trust you. You were in on the robbery and you fucked my closest man. You're a grimy bitch who can't be forgiven," I declare.

"But Ray, you're the only man I've ever loved romantically. AK took advantage of me when I was extremely vulnerable. You know me and the person who I am," Dionna narrates sincerely.

"And you're the only woman I've ever loved

romantically. We really had something. You made me believe in love. Before you, I was just jumping bitches off," I state.

"Right, so we both know we had something. We can move on from this and be better. AK is dead, so we won't have to deal with him being between us. It's you and me forever," Dionna vocalizes.

I reply, "You're right AK is dead and moving on doesn't sound like a bad idea. But one other thing. Tell me about the robbery."

"Like what about it?" Dionna inquires.

"Why did AK and you set me up to be robbed?" I ask.

"Well, AK was off his feet and he called you for a hookup and he was mad that you only offered five grand for him to get back on his feet," Dionna communicates.

I speak, "But, I was gonna link him with the ole boy. I told him that."

"I know, but once he heard the petty ass five grand, he was mad," Dionna tells.

"Then what happened?" I interrogate.

Dionna lowers her head and murmurs, "I jokingly said that he should rob you for the money."

"So basically you were joking and AK like he always does, took your statement and ran with it?" I ask.

"Yes, I didn't know he was even planning it. He left town out of the blue and was gone. Then he popped back up with mad money. I kept asking where he got money from and he eventually told me he had ya neighbors rob you," Dionna conveys.

"Damn, Baby. That makes me feel so much better. I was like ain't no way that you had something to do with it. AK used you," I state.

"Baby, you know I was fucked up over Dre's death, then you left, and then AK tells me you murdered him. I was lost and AK took advantage of me," Dionna communicates.

"I know he did and he used his friendship with me to do me dirty too," I say.

"Baby, we can get past this. I'll move on from you killing Dre and you move on from me and AK's affair," Dionna orates as she moves close to me.

Dionna goes to rest her head on my shoulder and I allow her to do so. She cries as she apologizes profusely. I love that she is truly showing contrition for her actions. I run my fingers through her hair and look her in the eyes.

I ask, "Can you do something to make this situation right for me Baby?"

"Yes, I can and will. Just name it and it's yours Ray. I promise," Dionna assures.

I speak as I push her away, "I need you to die bitch and die fast!"

Dionna's face quickly turns to one filled with befuddlement and horror. I raise the gun to her head immediately. I don't give her a chance to say one word.

"Good night bitch!" I say as I shoot Dionna in the head.

Dionna slumps over and falls dead on AK. I grab the bag with the drugs in it and sprinkle some of the coke on the dresser. I hope the cops think that their murders are related to these drugs. Next, I take AK's burner phone and exit the premises. I sneak back to my car and drive to Linden to link with my brother. I'm really not the one for driving with drugs in the car anymore, but I had no other choice. Once I find a way to dump these drugs, I'm out the game for good.

# Love this book and want more?

Visit RyanHodgeBooks.com

## More books by Ryan

The Deception Series:
*Web of Deception**
*Wrath of Deception**
*Will of Deception**
*Woes of Deception*
*Rape by Deception*****
*Workings of Deception* – Prequel to Web of Deception

Historical Science Fiction:
*Reversed World Power*
Urban Fiction
*Black Boy Lost, Black Girl Adrift*
Psychological Thriller
*Deadly Encounter*

*Adult romance
**Suspense Thriller.